"So what you're saying is to butt out of your business."

His jaw firmed for a moment and some unreadable emotion flashed in his eyes before he ground his teeth. "You want me to take off? Just say the word, and I'm out of here."

"No, please. That's not what I meant at all. I'm grateful for your protection."

"But you don't think you need it?"

"No, I do. It's just..." She sighed. "I don't know. Maybe it's more. You...me...there's something going on between us, right? And I don't want you to think just because you're stepping in to protect me that it's going anywhere."

He let his gaze linger. "So you feel it, too?"

"That's not the point."

"Isn't it?"

He had her there, but she wouldn't acknowledge it. She looked away again and felt his gaze on her, but she wouldn't turn back. He was right. It *was* the point. She didn't mind his taking Stan down a notch. In fact, she actually liked having someone on her side. Someone willing to defend her. And that was the problem, as she'd said. She couldn't—no, wouldn't—start to rely on someone for them to turn around and bail on her.

Susan Sleeman is a bestselling author of inspirational and clean-read romantic suspense books and mysteries. She received an RT Reviewers' Choice Best Book Award for *Thread of Suspicion*; *No Way Out* and *The Christmas Witness* were finalists for the Daphne du Maurier Award for Excellence. She's had the pleasure of living in nine states and currently lives in Oregon. To learn more about Susan, visit her website at susansleeman.com.

Books by Susan Sleeman

Love Inspired Suspense

First Responders

Silent Night Standoff
Explosive Alliance
High-Caliber Holiday
Emergency Response
Silent Sabotage

The Justice Agency

Double Exposure
Dead Wrong
No Way Out
Thread of Suspicion
Dark Tide

High-Stakes Inheritance
Behind the Badge
The Christmas Witness
Holiday Defenders
"Special Ops Christmas"

Visit the Author Profile page at Harlequin.com for more titles.

SILENT SABOTAGE

SUSAN SLEEMAN

HARLEQUIN® LOVE INSPIRED® SUSPENSE

Recycling programs
for this product may
not exist in your area.

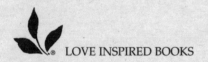

LOVE INSPIRED BOOKS

ISBN-13: 978-0-373-67768-9

Silent Sabotage

Copyright © 2016 by Susan Sleeman

www.Harlequin.com

Printed in U.S.A.

I have told you these things, so that in me you may
have peace. In this world you will have trouble.
But take heart! I have overcome the world.
–John 16:33

For my family, who always take over my responsibilities when I approach deadlines. It is through you and your patient understanding that I am able to share these stories of peace with readers.

ONE

The scream was high and sharp, and Emily felt her aunt Birdie's pain to her core.

"He's shooting at us!" Birdie cried.

Emily had heard the gunshots sounding from the parking lot at the flea market and antiques mall where they were shopping for all-natural soap. Could be a hunter, as cougar season was open all year in this part of Oregon, but the blasts sounded too close.

So then, what? A shooter on a killing spree? But that was ludicrous. Nothing like that happened in sleepy Bridal Veil, Oregon.

"Someone has to help us." Birdie took a tortured step back like a trapped animal ready to bolt.

"No one is shooting at us." Heart racing, Emily patted Birdie's arm and searched the space for any sign of a danger.

She saw a small crowd browsing at colorful booths rimming the exterior walls of the old grocery store. A mobile food cart selling corn dogs, pretzels and soda sat in the middle of the space next to worn picnic tables. Big fans whirred overhead, stirring the unusually steamy July air, but it was still thick and muggy. Nothing out of the ordinary for this small town in the foothills of Mount Hood, except the heat wave.

Emily lifted her hair from her sweaty neck, her heart rate starting to return to normal. She looked at Birdie, her face red and blotchy from the heat. In one of her Alzheimer's fogs, she'd insisted on wearing jeans and her favorite long-sleeved flannel shirt.

Pop, pop, pop. Gunfire rang out from the parking lot.

Birdie grabbed Emily's arm. "Did you hear that?"

"Yes." Emily spun toward the door, fear spearing her heart.

"A shooter!" a man yelled as he came running in the front door. "He's gone postal in the parking lot. He's headed this way."

"I told you so," Birdie said matter-of-factly as if being right was more important than the fact that a crazy gunman was coming into the building.

A burly guy stepped through the door with a big black rifle in his hands and green duffel bag slung over his shoulder. He wore a baseball cap pulled down low and surveyed the space. His jaw firmed in determination, and he looked up. Dark, cold eyes swept across the room.

"It's Delmar," Emily whispered, trying to stem her fear when she recognized the former member of Oregon Free, a local environmental group where she was a member.

Was he here for her?

He'd been kicked out of Oregon Free for committing violent acts to further environmental causes. Acts such as planning to blow up a bridge to stop tankers from carrying oil. Not that he was able to carry it out. He'd shared his plot with her to try to impress her so she'd go out with him, and she'd turned him in so the police could intercede before he caused unspeakable harm.

A sheriff's tactical team stormed the bridge, but Delmar's sister had already convinced him to hold a peaceful protest instead. When the authorities arrived, his anger surged, and he marched toward them. His sister tried to stop him before an officer shot him, but she caught her foot in a pothole and fell, hitting her head on the curb and dying on the spot.

An accident. A horrible accident. But Delmar blamed Emily for the death. Hated her. And now he was here with a gun. Likely for her.

Alarm bells rang in her head, and she started backing away, tugging Birdie with her.

"It's showtime, people," he shouted, lifting his weapon and staring at a young man holding a corn dog.

Delmar spoke to the man, and he replied as he backed away. Emily couldn't hear their conversation, but Delmar frowned, then lowered his eye to the sight and popped off a shot, cutting the man down.

Emily gasped and panic grabbed at her throat, making it hard to breathe.

Delmar swung his weapon up higher, his finger stretched out on the side. He ran the barrel over the crowd as if searching for someone specific. Back and forth he went, swinging in wide arcs until he stopped with the sight leveled in Emily's direction.

"We have to take cover," she whispered to Birdie and took her aunt's hand to slip quietly out of the aisle before he spotted her.

His steely eyes glared over the sight. He adjusted his cap, spit on the ground, then stepped into the food court. Up went the gun again. Down went his finger. He talked to two additional men, the result the same.

Stomp, stomp, stomp, he advanced on them. Heading her way.

Terror gripped Emily's body. They had to flee. Now! If he spotted her, he'd…

No. Not going there.

She turned to the nearest booth owner and whispered, "Is there a back door?"

"Yes, but you'll have to cross the courtyard to get there. He'll see you for sure." The owner melted into the corner of his space and ducked under a small table.

No room for Emily and Birdie to hide under there with him, but she couldn't keep moving and risk drawing Delmar's attention. She directed her aunt into the man's shop and behind a rack of soaps and lotions. Emily peeked around the rack to get a look at the food court.

Delmar came closer. Step by step. Bearing down on them.

Emily drew them deeper into the shadows and prayed. For herself. For Birdie. For everyone in the building. God was the only thing standing between them and a bullet.

Delmar stepped up to the booth and she confirmed his identity. His eyes were glazed and his focus jumpy. He'd had some run-ins with the law in violent protests, but he'd grown even more radical over the past few months. After his sister died, he'd also become bitter and angry. Now he was unhinged.

She waited. Watched him. His face. His expressions. The cold hate and fury emanating from his body. This wasn't the quiet and unassuming man she'd once sat beside in meetings. That she'd planned peaceful events with to save the environment.

This man, the one standing here, was filled with rage. His gaze connected with hers. Sharpened for a second, then narrowed into snake-like slits.

Emily's heart stuttered and nearly stopped beating.

"Emily Graves," he said, cocking his rifle, a sick smile sliding across his mouth. "Imagine finding you here…"

Boom. Boom. Boom.

Gunshots sounded from inside the mall as Deputy Archer Reed sneaked up on the main entrance. He might be alone, but as the first officer on scene, he had to take action, as it would be quite some time until reinforcements arrived. Twenty or so minutes outside the Portland metro area, deputies were spread thin. Even a rapid response team like his team wouldn't get there quickly enough. If he hadn't been driving back to Portland from doing a community outreach event when the active shooter call came over his radio, he wouldn't be here either. No law enforcement officer would be.

But he *was* here and it was up to him and him alone to stop the shooter.

He muted his radio so it didn't alert the shooter to his presence, then grabbed his rifle from the trunk of the squad car. Thankfully he'd come off patrol to go straight to the event so he was armed and ready to roll.

Strapping on his vest and grabbing extra ammo, he raced for the door, offering a prayer for the injured, the potential victims inside and for his ability to apprehend the shooter without loss of life.

He paused at the doorway to evaluate. The shooting had stopped, people had taken cover and it felt like a desert in the middle of summer. Jet engine–sized fans blew from above, stirring the muggy air. Loud and whiny, they would cover any sound he might make as he eased inside.

Muffled sounds, perhaps voices, came from a booth on the far side of the space. Archer raised his rifle and moved on the balls of his feet. Silently. Stealthily forward. Keeping to the edge of the booths.

Nearing the backside of the building, he saw movement in a shop with all-natural products made in Oregon.

A large man shot across the opening. Archer made him at five-ten, 180 pounds. Dark, ugly eyes. Holding a high-powered semiautomatic rifle in his hands and attired in a combat vest, the pockets holding fresh ammo clips.

Odd. Most active shooters wanted to die, but the vest, especially one with steel plates like the body armor he'd put on, said something else.

This guy was here to inflict damage—serious damage—and would not be easily taken out.

Sirens sounded in the distance. *Good.* Backup was almost there.

"I said do it. Now!" the shooter suddenly shouted. "Before the cops arrive."

Archer heard a woman respond. He couldn't make out her words, but she pled with the gunman as if he was holding her hostage.

A good sign, actually. If the shooter was taking hostages instead of opening fire, Archer could use his skills as a negotiator to talk him down. But first, Archer had to get close enough to evaluate the situation without alerting the gunman to his presence.

He dropped to the ground. Belly-crawled along the floor sticky with soda until he could see inside the booth. He forced himself to ignore the grime and focus on the action.

A woman with curly gray hair stood staring into the distance. A younger woman dressed in cutoff jean shorts and a bright yellow T-shirt stood tall in front of the older woman. A slight man wearing a brown shop apron huddled in the corner, his face slack, his mouth hanging open.

The shooter approached the young woman. Pressed the rifle barrel to her heart.

"Do as I ask or I'll shoot you right now."

"Delmar, please. I can't…"

Delmar. Something about that name rang a bell. Archer couldn't place it, but the woman knew the shooter's name.

Was she involved with him?

"My aunt." She turned to point at the older woman. "She's not well. Alzheimer's. She's afraid. Needs me by her side."

"Boo-hoo. I don't care. In front of me. *Now!*" He ground the rifle deeper into her chest.

After a lingering look at her aunt, the young woman complied and he clamped his arm around her neck, then backed away from the other people before releasing her. "Don't move."

Archer wanted the chance to use his negotiation skills to end this without loss of life, but right now, the situation still fell under an active shooter scenario and protocol called for an armed intervention.

He sighted his rifle on the gunman. Held his breath. Focused. No clear shot.

Weapon still trained on the woman, Delmar reached into a duffel bag sitting on a table and pulled out a bright red vest with pocketed explosives and long wires running from his backpack.

A suicide vest.

"Father, no," Archer whispered and drew in a breath.

"Put it on, Emily." Delmar's mouth split in a twisted smile. "I can think of no one better than you to wear this."

Emily. Her name was Emily, and she obviously knew the shooter but was terrified of him, and his piercing glare said he hated her.

What was going on here?

Large brown eyes flashing with strength and determination, she slipped her hands through the vest armholes. She stood five-six, and the vest hung to her thighs. The wires trailed along the floor to the backpack connecting her to Delmar.

Anger choked off Archer's breath, and he fought to draw in the sweltering air. How dare this shooter come in here, gun down innocent people and terrify this woman. How *dare* he!

He wasn't going to get away with it. Not today. Not on Archer's watch.

"Hurry it up. The cops are on the way just like I planned." Delmar grinned arrogantly. "But be careful. Wouldn't want to blow you to pieces… yet."

So he wanted the cops on scene and seemed as if he wanted to take Emily out, too. Maybe he was one of those guys who couldn't end his own life, and he needed the police to do it for him. Or…maybe this was designed as an ambush for responding officers.

Archer rolled to his side and scanned the building. Then to his back and other side, looking for a sniper waiting to kill the first responders. Archer didn't see anyone, but then if the shooter was a trained killer, Archer wouldn't see him.

"Why are you doing this, Delmar? Why me?" Emily's hand stilled over a Velcro loop and she looked up at Delmar. Her chin rose and her determination doubled when Archer expected her to fall apart or at the very least burst into tears.

A sardonic smile played on the man's face. "Why not you?"

"We once worked well together. Remember all the group meetings where we championed the same issues?"

Group? What group? Archer wanted to ask.

"Sure. Once upon a time." He paused, his face still filled with rage, then took a step closer. "That was before you killed my sister."

She looked up from fastening the vest's Velcro loops, terror in her brown eyes. "I didn't kill your sister. It was an accident. She fell and hit her head on the curb."

Delmar's lips curled in a sneer. "If you hadn't

reported my plan to the cops, Cindy would be alive today." He got in her face. "And you deserve to pay with your life. The world will be better off without you."

She gasped and stepped back, her worn Birkenstock sandals slapping on the concrete. "You can't mean that."

"I can and I do," Delmar bit out.

Archer cringed at the unfettered fear in her eyes now, but kept his focus glued to his scope. He was desperate to save this woman's life, yet he still hoped he wouldn't need to fire.

"You're not being fair," she said. "I was afraid your bomb at the bridge would take lives."

Bomb at the bridge.

Aha…that's it. How Archer knew the name *Delmar*. Though Archer wasn't the negotiator and hadn't responded with the First Response Squad to a bomb callout at the Interstate Bridge, he'd heard about the incident. Turned out there was no bomb, but a woman died in an unfortunate accident.

And Delmar, this man armed to kill, wanted revenge. On Emily. Maybe on the FRS for their response to the bridge callout.

A sick feeling sent acid burning up Archer's throat.

"I had to report you, don't you see?" Emily continued.

"And I have to end your life, don't you see?" He ended in a high note, mimicking her.

She gaped at him. "Is that what this is all about today? Shooting others to get to me?"

"Big head, much?" He rolled his eyes. "No, seeing you walk in the door just gave me a chance to stop trying to make your death look like an accident and take you out in a blaze of glory." He grinned, a mean, ugly smile. "Now close that vest so we can get on with my plans."

"What do you mean me dying by accident?" Her fingers shook as she finished the loops, then she raised her shoulders and stood staring at him, her arms hanging limply at her side.

"Exactly what I said. A pot rack falling in your kitchen. An arrow barely missing you, lodging in the tree instead."

Emily gasped. "You… Those…weren't accidents…? You did it? But when the police found a camouflage hat, they said the arrow was likely from a hunter who ran off because the season hadn't opened yet. They never thought someone had tried to kill me."

Delmar grinned, but didn't say another word. He drew out a trigger, the wires running straight to the bomb. Then he palmed the handheld trigger and proudly displayed it for the hostages.

Archer's heart sank. The guy had admitted

to trying to kill her, which could mean he had nothing to lose and planned to die today.

And was going to take himself and the hostages out with a bomb.

Emily took a step back, her gaze roaming the area. Her eyes locked on Archer. Before she could respond and give him away, he jerked out his badge and held it up for her to see then placed a finger over his mouth, telling her not to speak.

She took a deep breath then gave a jerky nod. Time stood still for a moment as he looked her in the eyes and transmitted confidence in his ability to end this standoff successfully. And before he looked away, he caught a flash of renewed strength in her eyes. She was a strong, courageous woman, and he was looking forward to meeting her once this was all over.

Archer returned to his scope. Fixed it on Delmar, then zoomed in to get a better look at the bomb trigger.

Archer wasn't the bomb tech on the First Response Squad, but he'd seen his fair share of devices, and the unit in Delmar's hand looked like a compression switch.

This wasn't good. Not good at all.

If Delmar was shot or simply released his hand, the bomb would detonate.

Oh, man.

The game had dramatically changed. Not only was Emily—a woman Delmar hated and wanted dead—now his hostage, but he could take out the whole building with the simple release of his fingers.

TWO

Archer stood before Delmar Withrow and the hostages. After seeing the bomb, he'd crawled out to notify dispatch that they were now in a hostage situation and to prevent arriving officers from rushing the building and firing on Withrow. Then he'd called the FRS and pocketed his phone to keep his connection with team leader Jake Marsh so he and the team could listen in.

Archer had already gotten introductions out of the way with Withrow when he'd announced his presence over a bullhorn. Withrow demanded Archer leave his gun at the door before stepping inside to talk. Archer had no choice, and he'd complied.

Before he started negotiating, he quickly glanced at Emily to restore their earlier connection. He couldn't hold her gaze for more than a second, but that was all it took to see her confidence in him.

Good. She was calm enough not to be a danger to herself or others.

He turned his attention to Withrow to start by asking for something in good faith. "I'd like to bring in medics to tend to the wounded."

The gunman arched a bushy brow. "What's in it for me?"

Right. He really didn't care about the hostages. Not surprising. Archer resisted gritting his teeth. "If you don't take this any further, your prison time will be greatly reduced."

Withrow held up the trigger. "What makes you think I'm planning on going to prison instead of letting this go?"

"You should consider it as an option."

"Maybe." A sick grin slid across his lips. "Once my demands are met."

Now they were getting somewhere.

Archer kept the hope for a peaceful resolution from his voice and spoke in Withrow's deadpan tone. "Demands?"

"Quit trying to yank my chain." Withrow scowled. "I know you're here to try to talk me out of this, but you won't. You have to know by my actions that I'm committed to my cause and will stop at nothing for my voice to be heard."

"This isn't the way to do it," Emily said matter-of-factly.

Withrow glared at her. "A real advocate of environmental causes would be here applauding me. Helping me. Not antagonizing me."

She gaped at him. "Do you really think anyone in Oregon Free would support murdering people?"

"Some would."

"How do you know that?" she prompted.

"Because we discussed it."

"So others know about this…your plan to kill people?" she asked.

"Maybe." He grinned.

So he had people supporting him. One. Two. Possibly more? Could these accomplices have helped him with those other so-called accidents he'd mentioned, too?

Archer hated relinquishing control of the conversation to Emily, but getting the guy on record admitting his crimes would help in keeping him behind bars, so Archer would stand back unless this turned ugly.

"Stan's working with you, right?" she prodded. "He and Cindy were engaged, and I know he's mad at me. Did he help you with the arrow and pot rack, too?"

"Really, Emily? You think I'm going to tell you."

"You felt free to say you'd tried to kill me," she pointed out. "Why not tell me if you had help?"

"I have nothing to lose." He held out the trigger, raising Archer's apprehension. "Not after this. But I won't implicate those who can carry on my mission."

Archer could feel the hatred radiating from the creep. Emily was the enemy and he had friends standing behind him. Even if Archer succeeded in resolving this safely and putting Withrow behind bars, would the others continue their attacks on her?

"You mentioned a cause," Archer said. "Tell me about it."

Withrow swung his gaze back to Archer. "It's about time someone asked. Big Oil is trying to transport three hundred and sixty thousand barrels of oil a day through the Columbia River Gorge. Railroad cars loaded with the stuff. I aim to stop it today."

Archer was familiar with the contentious battle with the corporation that'd built a large oil depot just across the state line and hoped to transport oil in a mobile pipeline.

"I would think you'd go straight to the oil company and place your demands there," Archer continued in a calm, steady voice. "How can shooting up a mall help?"

"Just like a cop." Contempt tightened Withrow's eyes. "Can't see the obvious. Security at the oil company is like trying to break into Fort Knox, and I'd get nowhere."

"Still doesn't explain the mall."

"Couldn't resist the chance to pay back my so-called neighbors who are supporting the pipeline. And, of course, this…" he paused and held up the trigger "…wouldn't have been possible in the city. Cops would be breathing down my neck before I got the vest out of the bag. But out in the country you cops are few and far between."

He was right. Many Oregon counties had lost funding and had to cut back on law enforcement. This county was no exception.

"Now," Withrow continued, "you're going to get a TV reporter on site to film this so people will sit up and take notice and finally stand up to the stinking oil company."

"So you want to speak to a reporter?" Archer clarified.

"Yeah. Get one out here to do an interview, and I'll turn over the trigger."

Archer didn't trust that Withrow's motives were as pure as he was making it sound, but Archer could use the demand to negotiate for the evacuation of the wounded. "You allow the medics to tend to the innocents you wounded and transport them to the ER, and I'll work on arranging your interview."

Withrow arched an eyebrow. "I only plugged three guys and all of them deserved it."

"You expect me to believe that?"

"You mean that they deserved it? Yeah. They've supported Big Oil and it was about time someone made them pay."

"I meant with all the bullets you fired, that you only hit three people?"

"It's the truth." He waved the trigger device at Emily. "This was my end game all along."

"In that case, you'll let the medics in," Archer stated.

"The guys deserved what they got, but..." He shrugged. "If letting the medics haul them out gets me what I want, then so be it. I'll provide the location of the first two and if the reporter isn't here by then, number three will have to wait."

Of course, he would arrange this to meet his needs alone. "I have to get out my phone to call my supervisor."

"Go ahead."

Archer dug out his phone. Not that the call mattered at all other than to assuage Withrow, as Jake would never let a reporter come into a standoff.

As Archer talked, Withrow stepped to his backpack and traded his rifle for a handgun. He circled around Emily and jerked her against his chest. He pressed the gun against her temple.

Archer expected her to blanch or even get

sick, but she stood strong through his call and while the medics removed two of the injured.

"Okay, Nee-go-tiator," Withrow sneered. "Seein's how you didn't comply with my demand, I'll give you another thirty minutes. I see a reporter or I detonate the bomb."

"You don't want to do this, Delmar," Archer said in a flat tone. "You heard the medics. The people you shot were still alive. So why not do this the smart way? You don't need to die today."

"This's the only way I get to talk to a reporter."

"Not so. I can get on the phone right now and arrange for an interview for you once you surrender."

"Right." Delmar's brow creased. "You'd arrest me and then not follow through."

"Even if I did—" Archer paused and looked him square in the eye "—which I won't—you don't have to rely on me. You control the people who visit you in County lockup. Put any or every reporter you can think of on your visitor list and they'll be glad to come see you. That way your message will be broadcast on more than one station."

He raised an eyebrow. "I could, couldn't I?"

"Sure. Plus, if you direct us to the last guy, you won't go away for murder and can get out so much sooner to continue your quest to protect the environment."

"Maybe," he said and his arm slackened from around Emily's neck.

"Not only that," Archer added, making sure he sounded enthusiastic, "you can continue fighting for your cause from prison. You can't do that if you release the trigger."

Archer could see he was making progress and it was time to end the standoff. "Who's going to take up the charge if you're not here? No one's as passionate about it as you are. Don't you want to keep fighting?"

"I do."

Archer slowly lifted his arm and held out his hand. "Then give me the remote, and I'll make sure the reporter comes to visit you."

Withrow took a halting step forward.

Yes...

Then another step.

It was all Archer could do not to rush the guy, but he stayed put, his feet planted firmly on the ground.

Withrow took the remaining steps. Held out the trigger. Archer wrapped his hand around it and freed it from Withrow.

The room seemed to sigh in relief.

"Now on the floor, hands behind your back," Archer said in a nonthreatening tone when every part of him wanted to bark orders at the man.

Withrow's expression changed, and he looked as if he was going to balk.

"Your cause," Archer soothed as he might with a small child. "Remember your cause."

Withrow gave a firm nod, then lay down.

Wearing tactical gear, the First Response Squad flooded the room. Archer held firm on the trigger and looked at Emily. A grateful smile played across her lips, and if he wasn't already captivated by her incredible bravado under pressure, her smile was enough to suck him in and never let him go.

The deputy named Archer who saved them all crossed over to Emily. He'd risked his life coming into this building to rescue them. Took a fine man to do that and she wanted to fling her arms round his neck and express her thanks. But she still wore the vest and until she was out of it, this wasn't over for her.

"The vest. Can I take it off now, please?" she implored, as chaos seemed to reign around her with men in black clothes, helmets and heavy vests hauling Delmar to his feet.

Archer shook his head regretfully. "Our bomb expert will be in soon to take the trigger and help you."

"How long will that be?"

"He's suiting up now. I know these guys look

kind of intimidating in their tactical attire, but if you haven't done anything wrong you have nothing to worry about."

She shot him a look. "Do you think I'm involved in this? Because I assure you I'm not."

He shrugged as if he dealt with incidents like this every day. Maybe he did, but she sure didn't. "I know Delmar, yes, but as you heard he hates me and apparently wants to kill me."

"Yeah, I heard, and it sounds like you were just in the wrong place at the wrong time, but it's not up to me to figure out your role. Once you're free of the bomb, we'll turn this over to detectives to sort out and my team and I will take off."

"No!" she said before thinking about it. "Please. You saw me through this so far… Can't you stay? Just for a little while."

She sounded weak and whiny but she didn't care. She was still wearing a vest. A bomb vest, for goodness' sake! And people had been gunned down right in front of her. *Unbelievable.*

She didn't think she'd ever forget what she'd seen and heard today. How could life ever go back to normal? Especially if Stan was coming after her to kill her. This handsome deputy standing tall and strong beside her, the man who risked his life for her, gave her hope that she desperately needed right now.

"Please," she added when he didn't speak.

A muscle ticked in his jaw. "Let me go talk to my team leader." He took powerful strides across the space and stopped by a man who removed his helmet.

The leader clapped Archer on the back. "Great work, Archer."

Archer.

She liked the name. Kind of regal and formal, which seemed to fit him. At times, there was something in his expression that was warm and welcoming, and yet there was an undercurrent of steel and a warning not to mess with him.

He looked every bit the rescuer, too. He was very tall, six foot four maybe, long and lean, but solidly built. A square jaw, sandy brown hair cut short and a uniform that fit to a T added to her perception. His eyes were icy blue and they seemed to look right through people.

He also seemed like a man who liked to control the action.

Just her type. Which meant if she crossed paths with him ever again, she'd turn and run in the other direction, as she wasn't getting involved with any man. Ever.

She jerked her focus away and watched as two men snapped cuffs on Delmar and hauled him to his feet before marching him forward.

"Easy now," he bellowed. "You'll pay for every bruise I find."

At his approach, he glared at her, his eyes a mass of anger and resentment. His narrow lips curled up in a wicked smile. His dark, sinister stare remained locked on her.

She cringed and wanted to scoot back from the barely contained rage, but that's what he wanted, so she stayed strong.

His smile turned into a smirk. "You may have won this round, but our fight is far from over, *sweetheart*. And if I were you, I'd watch your back."

THREE

Emily sat at a folding table under a canopy in the mall's parking lot. Birdie rested at a similar table twenty feet away. A vacant, empty expression born from jumbled memories claimed her aunt's face. Emily had asked to stay with Birdie and offer comfort, but Detective Carothers, who would investigate the case, forbid them to talk to each other until after they'd given their statements.

Poor Birdie. Stuck here. Alone. Lost and confused.

A common problem these days. Hour after hour. Day after day. Confusion. Fear. Living in another world. All courtesy of Alzheimer's, early stage two. If they could afford a care nurse, Emily would have left her aunt home today. If it hadn't been absolutely necessary, Emily wouldn't have come either, but upcoming guests were expecting to find all-natural soap at the environmentally friendly B and B, and ordering soap was just one of the things that had fallen through the cracks as she desperately tried to save the business.

The fund-raiser. She'd almost forgotten. They'd scheduled a mini-carnival for that night to raise a quick influx of cash to pay the mortgage. If they failed, Birdie would be out of business in short order. Plus, Emily had invested all of her savings in the business, so if it went under, she and her aunt would be homeless and penniless.

Emily checked her watch. She had to get out of there and quickly. She searched the area for Detective Carothers, who was deep in conversation with Archer and his team leader, Jake Marsh. The detective, a pencil-thin man wearing a baggy suit, clutched a folder to his chest and locked Jake in a stare down. Jake appeared to be asking for something.

Carothers suddenly shoved his hand into his hair and gave a firm nod. He spun, then started toward her. Jake gave Archer a thumbs-up. Archer grinned.

"Ms. Graves." A sour look claimed Detective Carothers's face as he dropped into one of the metal folding chairs across the table. "Deputies Marsh and Reed will be sitting in with us, but I'll be taking lead on this investigation."

"I don't mean to sound impertinent, but could

you wait to take my statement?" she asked, and explained about the fund-raiser and how important it was to their business. "If I don't get going now, we won't be ready on time."

"I need to take your statement while the incident is fresh in your mind."

Archer took a step toward Carothers. "Why not cut Ms. Graves some slack? She could jot down her thoughts right now, and you could question her later at home. Withrow is off the streets and won't hurt anyone, so this isn't time sensitive."

Carothers pressed his lips together. "That is against protocol."

"I get that," Archer said. "But sometimes we need to be flexible."

"She could talk to others. Change her story."

"Look," Archer added, "I'll be glad to accompany her home and keep an eye on her all night. If someone is helping Withrow get back at her, I can keep her safe and ensure she doesn't talk to anyone about the incident. Then if you have questions, I'll personally escort her to the station in the morning or you can come to the B and B if you'd rather do it that way."

Carothers took a long breath, let it out, then shoved a legal pad and pen across the table to her.

"Write down your version of the incident,

leaving nothing out, and you can go." He stood, gestured for Deputy Marsh to follow him and stepped away from the table.

She looked up at Archer. "Thank you. Normally, I wouldn't put you out like this, but the fund-raiser is basically our last chance to keep Birdie's B and B afloat."

"I don't mind." He sounded sincere and his eyes were warm and friendly. "Besides, it seems like you could use some help getting ready for the fund-raiser, and I'm nothing if not helpful."

He turned on a megawatt smile, and she had to look away before she found herself smiling up into eyes that were at times icy blue and like now, a warm, soothing baby blue. The last thing she needed was for him to think she was one of the many dopey-eyed women who must fall at his feet all the time.

She didn't want to date anyone or even engage in a flirtation. Her mind needed to be squarely on helping Birdie. That, and if Delmar's threat was true, watching her own back so she stayed alive to take care of her aunt.

Archer trailed Emily Graves's classic pickup truck around another bend and onto a gravel road lined with tall pine trees. The temperature had dropped and the once-vibrant sunshine disappeared, replaced with heavy shadows moving in the breeze.

As they approached the B and B, an uneasy feeling settled in his gut. His agency patrolled the large county with both urban and rural areas, but he'd never worked the rural beat. Coming from cosmopolitan New York City, where he'd lived his entire life, he was far more comfortable in a city setting than a rural one.

He followed Emily another three miles over hills, around bends, and she finally clicked on her blinker near a large house set back from the road. She turned the rusty truck under a blistered white sign with Birdie's Bed-and-Breakfast etched in black lettering hanging from large log poles over a dirt-packed driveway. They wound around a few curves until he spotted a guest-parking sign near a small paved lot, but Emily gestured out her window to follow her toward the house.

Two stories, the place was painted a cheerful yellow with white trim, but as he drove closer, he could see the building needed a fresh coat of paint. A wide wraparound porch held white wooden rocking chairs and large planters filled with red and purple flowers. Off to the side of the house, he spotted a small cottage painted in matching colors with window boxes overflowing with the same flowers.

Emily suddenly stopped, and Archer had to slam on his brakes not to rear-end her truck. She jumped out and rounded the front of her car before bending down and disappearing from sight.

A spear of adrenaline sliced into his body, and he charged across the space to check on her. He was aware of Birdie getting out of the car and mumbling, but his focus remained on Emily. He reached the front of her vehicle, and she stood, her back to him.

"What's wrong?" he asked, trying to keep the concern from his voice.

She turned and was holding a coffee-colored chicken with white tail feathers. "Birdie left the chicken coop open again."

"Did not," Birdie said, but Archer suspected she wouldn't remember if she had.

"Here." Emily shoved the chicken into his hands and let go.

"What…" Archer complained, but Emily was already chasing after another chicken running toward the road.

Archer gaped after her. What in the world was he supposed to do with a chicken? His only experience with chickens was in a dining room, and he hadn't a clue what to do with a living bird.

It squirmed and squawked in his hands, and

he held it out as he searched for a place to get rid of it. Instead, he found five more chickens pecking the ground and scurrying around. He searched for Birdie, but she'd ignored the fiasco and was climbing the wide steps to the house.

So he stood like a dolt, hands outstretched until Emily returned with her fingers around the wayward chicken's feet, the body clutched against her side and the head tucked under her arm.

"Follow me and hold that chicken this way." She lifted her arm. "Or she's going to squirm out of your hands."

He tried maneuvering the plump bird, but she clucked loudly so he held her as close as he could and trailed Emily. She zigzagged around the yard, corralling the other birds. Together, they all clipped across the clearing and down a hill toward a small weatherworn building. It sat on raised stilts with a side room made of wooden uprights and covered in chicken wire. Emily scooted the chickens through a door into the open area, then slipped the one she was holding into the space.

Good. Archer could get rid of this animal, too. He rushed forward, maybe too fast for the bird, and made it nervous as it deposited a big splotch of white-and-brown gunk on his shirt.

"Ack," he shouted and held out the chicken.

Emily watched him for a moment, then started laughing.

"It's not funny," he warned sternly. "This is my uniform, and I don't want it ruined even more than it already is from the mall."

"You're right. The shirt isn't funny, and I'm sorry this happened." Her grin widened. "But you stared down a guy with a bomb not more than an hour ago with hardly a hint of what you were feeling, and now? Now the horror on your face is from a chicken. That's priceless."

"I'm not a country guy, all right?" He shoved the bird at her.

"That goes without saying." She cradled the chicken and settled it in the building. "If she was making an egg, the way you held her would surely be the end of that."

Archer didn't care about an egg. He looked down on his shirt and gagged. He quickly undid the buttons and rubbed the offending gook onto the grass. He wore a khaki-colored T-shirt to match his uniform shirt, but it had a moist spot as well so he held it away from his body.

Emily turned and when her gaze landed on him, she stopped in her tracks and peered at him. The humor was long gone in her expression, and she stared at him with a clear look of interest.

If he wasn't so creeped out about the goo on his shirt, he suspected he'd be returning the gaze, but this mess outweighed most everything else. "Is there somewhere I can clean up? I've got clothes in my trunk, but I'm not putting them on until I wash up."

"I can wash your shirt." She held out her hand.

He gladly turned it over. "I'll grab my clothes."

He sensed her watching him as he walked back to his car and could just imagine what she was thinking. He was a deputy. Could carry a gun and shoot people. Was trained in defensive combat and worked out to keep in top physical shape, and yet, a little bit of bird poop and he'd acted like a big sissy.

He didn't like it any more than she did, but he was raised with overly strict cleanliness standards and, try as he might, he'd never been able to relax them. His pants and shirts were pressed at all times. If he got a spot on them, even a small one, he changed. Sure, it was prissy, but it was ingrained, and he made no apologies.

He grabbed his duffel bag and met Emily on the front porch. Without a word, but the remaining hint of a smile on her face, she escorted him straight to an upstairs bathroom.

"Do you need a full shower or will a washcloth with soap and water suffice?" Her eyes creased with unspoken laughter.

"No shower necessary," he retorted and didn't mind one bit that she gave him a knowing look as she shut the bathroom door.

In fact, he kind of found her teasing cute and endearing.

Odd.

He sure didn't react that way when the team razzed him about his cleanliness obsession. Although he didn't like it coming from them, for some reason this was different. He was sure that if he examined his feelings, he might discover the underlying cause, but in his mind, this situation was best left unexplored.

He ripped off his undershirt and scrubbed his stomach clean before putting on the fresh FRS uniform of a black polo shirt and tactical pants that he always kept at the ready. When he stepped back into the hallway, Emily was waiting for him.

She held out her hand. "I can add the undershirt to the washer, too."

For a moment, he froze as it seemed so personal to be handing an undershirt to a near stranger, but like it or not, he'd rather the stain be removed.

"I can help," he offered.

"You want to help because you don't trust me to get it clean enough." She grinned up at him.

"Busted," he said and found himself smiling

back at her. "Also, I came here to help, not add to your workload."

"Please." She rolled her eyes. "It's taking us longer to talk about this than it will take to do it."

"Then would you mind if I have a look around the place while you put it in the washer? I want to check out the security."

Her smile fell. "Security. Why?"

"I promised to make sure you remained safe, and I always keep my promises."

"Oh, I heard you all right when you said that. You also said you'd keep an eye on me all night, but that's not going to happen."

"I meant that figuratively, but make no mistake, Ms. Graves, I'll be staying here all night."

She narrowed her eyes. "On the couch."

He refrained from dropping his mouth open at her innuendo. "I'm here to protect you and nothing more."

"I didn't…" She shook her head and ran her fingers through long, chocolate-brown waves. "Do you really think one of Delmar's friends is going to come after me?"

"It's too early to tell," he said to keep from heightening her apprehension. "But threats have been issued and we have to take them seriously until we can prove them false."

"Understood," she said, suddenly looking distracted. "I'll get the laundry started, then meet you on the porch when you finish your tour."

"Are there any rooms off-limits?"

"We don't have guests right now, but I suspect Birdie might be napping. Her room is on the third floor in the front. If the door is closed she's asleep, and I'd appreciate it if you didn't disturb her."

"You got it."

She looked at him as if pondering something, then turned and started down the hallway. Maybe he wasn't able to read all of her expressions, but one thing was clear. She was uneasy around him, and she didn't try to hide it. He'd tried to be compassionate and understanding so he wasn't giving off a tough-deputy vibe, but there was obviously something else that bothered her.

Maybe he wasn't doing a very good job of hiding the way she piqued his curiosity. Or maybe, she was just out of her element with everything that had happened.

Archer watched her disappear in the stairwell. He'd read in her statement that she was an accountant and he tried to imagine her in that position. With his MBA, he understood the duties in an accounting job, and he honestly couldn't see her spending her days inside, bent over a desk in a small cubicle.

Problem was, he wanted to know more about her so he *could* figure out where she belonged.

"Get a grip," he mumbled as he started his tour. "Remember why you're here."

He searched five guest rooms and three bathrooms, all decorated in a traditional style to match the age of the house. The windows and locks were original, and it wouldn't take much to jimmy them open. Hopefully, the first-floor windows had better locks.

Archer climbed creaky stairs to the third floor, where the temperatures spiked and any attempt at decorating stopped. He suspected these were once servants' quarters.

One door was closed, and he heard a fan running from inside. Birdie's room, he supposed. He walked through a small sitting room with a table holding a reading lamp and piled high with books. He went into the other bedroom, and the wildly colored clothing hanging on a portable clothes rack, much like the bright hue of Emily's shirt today, told him it was her room. The furniture was period and all looked original, especially the worn sofa against the far wall and the tall highboy in the corner. Water stained the upper portion of the plaster wall behind her ornate headboard and large sections of plaster had been removed, exposing the studs.

Archer suspected they'd opened the wall to

fix a plumbing leak and never finished the repair. Her window was open with a box fan running on high speed, but it was still stifling hot in here, and he left the room before he started sweating in his clean shirt.

He took the stairway to the main floor. The dark wood was old and worn, but polished until it gleamed. The living area held comfortable furniture and walls filled with shelves packed with books.

Clean, tidy and spotless like the other rooms. He'd been impressed with Emily before, but her penchant for neatness added to the appeal.

The locks were of the same flimsy nature as the upper floors, and he didn't like that one bit. Frowning to himself, he stepped into the kitchen and climbed up on a chair to look at the beam holding the pot rack. He spotted roughly patched holes, likely where it hung before and had been moved over a few inches. Archer saw nothing to suggest Withrow caused the rack to fall, but then with the original holes patched, Archer didn't think he would. He pulled hard on the rack just to be sure it was securely fastened, and once he was satisfied, he finished his inspection before stepping onto the porch, where Emily gazed over the property, a clipboard in hand.

A cool, soft breeze played over his skin. The temperature in the secluded location was far cooler than the city and the steaming-hot grocery store. She'd tidied up a bit, pulling her hair up into a ponytail, giving her a girl-next-door look. She seemed so sweet and innocent, so far removed from the catty socialites he'd met when he'd lived in New York. Maybe that's why she sparked his interest.

She pointed at a large truck in the driveway. "The workers just got here with the bouncy house and other games. Would you mind overseeing the setup to make sure they put them in the right location?"

"Sure, tell me where they go and I'm all over it."

She pulled a very detailed map from her clipboard.

He studied it. "When do you need these ready to go?"

"An hour."

"Okay, you got it." He set an alarm on his watch.

"My timing isn't *that* precise."

"Time is money, you know," he said, issuing one of his favorite quotes. "You can count on me to have it all ready within an hour."

She eyed him for a few seconds. "Let me know if you have any issues."

She jogged down the stairs, her ponytail bouncing. Made her look carefree, but with her struggle to keep the B and B afloat and the incident this afternoon, she was clearly anything but.

He got that. If she was right about this Stan guy, she had to be worried about another attack. At least Archer was concerned, and only one way to put it out of his head. A visit to Stan Fannon, which he would do first thing in the morning.

FOUR

The afternoon flew by and Emily couldn't believe she'd managed to get everything organized for the small carnival. She wouldn't have been able to do it without Archer. He pitched in wherever needed, and that included the last item on her list, gathering eggs from the coop so she could sell them. She'd built rollout nest boxes that would allow him simply to open the back to retrieve eggs without entering the coop or sticking his hand under a chicken, but he still puckered his lips as he started gathering.

She forced her mind from those lips that she suspected had kissed many women and went over her list one more time. She realized she hadn't seen Birdie for some time so she went to check on her and found her in the kitchen eating a large bowl of cereal.

Emily watched her aunt from the door for a few moments. She had a mop of wild, curly hair that she'd clipped up in the back, leaving tendrils sticking out in every direction. She'd changed into striped capris and a short-sleeved blue T-shirt much more in keeping with the warm temps.

She suddenly looked up and noticed Emily. The smile Emily treasured slid across Birdie's face and brought tears to Emily's eyes. She had to cherish each and every one of these smiles, as there were fewer and fewer of them as time passed.

"Hi, sweetie," she said, her eyes clear and present in the moment.

Emily's heart lifted at the return of her aunt. "The fund-raiser is all set up. Why don't you come out and have some fun for a change?"

"I'm way too tired to attend." She yawned and stretched. "I'm going to finish up my cereal and go to bed."

Concerned, Emily stepped inside. "You're not feeling ill are you?"

Birdie shook her head, her curls springing in every direction. "Stop worrying about me. Go enjoy the event you worked so hard to prepare, and I'll be fine."

"We do have a nice crowd building out there. I'm sure we'll raise at least enough money for another loan payment."

Birdie frowned and pushed back from the table. "I'm sorry I put you in this position."

"It's not your fault, and I won't have you worrying about it." Emily squeezed her aunt's shoulders. "I'll save some of the goodies for you so you can have them for lunch tomorrow."

Birdie clutched Emily's hand, as tears started to glisten in her own eyes. "I don't know what I'd do without you."

Memories of walking through the same back door with a small suitcase and a broken heart washed over Emily. More tears threatened, but she forced them back and smiled. "Then we're even. I had the same feeling many years ago when I came to live with you. Who knows what would have happened to me without your love and support. Now it's my turn to give back."

"Thank you for being so gracious." Birdie gave Emily's hand a kiss then released it. "Now scoot."

Emily didn't move. She wanted to stay. To enjoy the time when Birdie's memory was so clear. To just bask in her aunt's presence and enjoy the only person who'd loved her unconditionally. How she was going to miss the warmth, the affection when Birdie's memory had been fully eclipsed.

She grabbed Birdie in a hug and held tight.

"Now, now," Birdie cooed. "Everything's going to be all right."

No, it wouldn't. Birdie would forget everything, even basic bodily functions, and Emily would be all alone unless she did something about it. But what could she do? Men were off-limits. She'd been raised in a highly dysfunctional and chaotic home. An alcoholic father who caroused and had affairs. A mother who paid him back with affairs of her own and didn't bother to hide them. They fought all the time. Bickering. Snapping. Mean, ugly fights.

When the arguing got brutal, Emily had learned to take control of her own life. To go to the library or when it was closed to take a stroll through the park. Then her father took off and when Emily was thirteen, her mother chose a man who didn't want children. So her mother left Emily on Birdie's doorstep. Life might have been tough and her mother less than the parent Emily had wanted, but she was her mother and Emily had grieved her leaving like a death in the family.

Emily vowed then and there that she would never be hurt again. And to make sure that didn't happen, she took control of everything. Of herself. Her surroundings. And she never… *never*…gave her heart to a man as her mother had done so many times.

Better to live alone as Birdie had all of her life. It had worked so far, and Emily was happier than her mother and father ever were. She wasn't about to change that now. Especially for a man whose smile reminded her of all the men her mother readily gave in to.

Emily kissed Birdie's papery cheek and went back outside just in time to see Archer come up the hill with a full basket of eggs. They were basically clean but had a few feathers and bits of shavings on them.

Not that Archer noticed. He had that same puckered expression lingering on his handsome face. "I imagine you want me to wash these before you sell them."

"Washing eggs can allow bacteria to get inside the shell." She grabbed a rag sitting by the empty cartons and handed it to him. "Just wipe the outside and put them in the cartons."

His pucker grew, and she had to fight back a laugh. He was obviously a clean freak, and he was torn between handling the eggs again and running in the other direction.

"I can do it if you don't want to," she offered.

He shook his head hard and firmed his brow in determination. "No. I got it."

The thought of having a guy around who put her needs first as he'd been doing brought a trickle of joy and she forced it away. The last thing she needed was to be beholden to this man.

"FYI," he added. "Jake just texted me with

an update on the shooting victims. Two are in stable condition and should be released soon."

"And the other one?"

He frowned. "In surgery. He lost a lot of blood and is in critical condition."

"Then he needs our prayers more than ever," she replied softly, vowing to redouble her efforts to pray on his behalf. "Will Deputy Marsh keep you updated if anything changes?"

Archer nodded. "And as soon as I know anything I'll make sure you know, too." He lifted the basket. "I'll get these done so I can help you with something else."

She stepped away to find a quiet spot to pray, but turned back to check on him. Oddly enough, she was proud that he was able to clean and carton the eggs. A simple task for sure, but he'd done something he detested. Something for her and Birdie. A pure, selfless act. Sure, it was only boxing up eggs, but outside of the guys on the FRS today, no man had really put himself in an uncomfortable position for her, and she was touched that he continued to do so.

His generosity temporarily erased the bad day, allowing her to breeze through her tasks. Unfortunately, once the carnival was in full swing, Detective Carothers cut across the grass, ending her good mood. Archer hurried over to join him. They held a heated conversation, before they stepped up to her.

"Detective Carothers felt he needed to talk to you tonight," Archer announced, his lips thinning in disapproval.

"My lieutenant insisted," Carothers said. "We still need to look for accomplices and document the incident."

"Accomplices?" She watched him for a moment. "You think because we were once part of the same group that I helped him, don't you?"

Carothers leveled his gaze at her. "Did you?"

"I may know Delmar from Oregon Free, but I am not friends with him and would never help him or anyone else shoot innocent people, much less willingly wear a bomb vest."

"Then why don't we find someplace quiet and away from the crowd so you can tell me why you were at the mall today?"

"Good idea," she huffed. "I'd like to get this cleared up once and for all. Follow me." Emily led the way to a long picnic table down by their guest cottage. It sat in the middle of a gazebo covered with fragrant honeysuckle and was lit with sparkling white Christmas tree lights. She took a seat on the nearest bench.

Carothers sat across from her. Archer leaned a broad shoulder on an upright and crossed his ankles. On the surface, he looked relaxed and carefree, but she could see frustration lingering in his eyes. He was just as unhappy about Carothers's untimely visit as she was.

Carothers flipped open his notebook. "Now, why were you at the mall?"

"As I put in my statement, a simple shopping trip," she replied. "We needed soap for our guest bathrooms. We've recently made a name for ourselves as an all-natural inn and the mall is the only place close by that sells the soap we use."

"So you didn't know Delmar Withrow was going to be there?"

"No. Like I said, we're not friends or anything, so how would I know that?"

"In fact, from your statement, it sounds like he hates you."

She sighed. "I knew he blamed me for his sister's death. That word spread around town fast, but the Oregon Free group kicked him out for his violent behavior, so I haven't seen him since then. And before you ask, I didn't know that the incidents that happened here weren't accidents."

"Why don't you tell us more about them," Archer said, earning a raised eyebrow from Carothers.

She swiveled to look up at him. "First, we had this large cast iron pot rack above the island in the kitchen. I was making sandwiches on the island one day when my phone rang. It was on the table so I stepped away to answer it. Just as I did, the rack fell. If I hadn't moved, it would have hit me." A shudder racked her body, but she ignored it. "In case you haven't noticed, this place is in desperate need of repairs so we thought it was just one of the many items that needed to be fixed. Now Delmar claims he was behind it."

"Not sure how he could know that it would hit you," Carothers stated.

"True. It could have fallen at any time, but I'm the only one who cooks here so if it did hit anyone, it would be me."

"And it would look like an accident if Delmar rigged it the right way," Archer added.

"I'd like to see it."

"I already checked it out," Archer informed the detective. "The handyman repaired the holes and put in new bolts. There's nothing to see there."

"And the other incident?" Carothers asked.

She swung her attention back to him. "A few weeks later, I was in the garden just over the hill. I bent down to harvest a head of lettuce when an arrow flew over me, then lodged in a tree. If I hadn't bent over…" She let her words fall off because she couldn't say aloud that she now believed the incident was on purpose.

"And you said you called this in and it was determined that someone was hunting out of season and took off," Archer added.

She nodded, but didn't look at him. "But now it also looks like Delmar's handiwork." She shook her head. "This is all so unbelievable. I'm a corporate accountant. Or at least I was until I came back to help Birdie with the B and B. I sat in a cubicle. Ran numbers. Hardly a job where someone might try to use a bow and arrow to kill me."

"Do you remember the date and time of these incidents?" Carothers asked.

"No," she replied. "But the police report will have it for the arrow, right?"

"Right," Archer said, then looked at Carothers. "If Withrow really is behind this, then we'll need to see if he's bow hunted in the past and if he has an alibi for that day."

There was that *we* thing again. Was he really going to stay beyond today?

Carothers puffed up his chest and eyed Archer. "*I'll* be doing just that. Since hunting licenses don't fall under our jurisdiction it might take some time to get my hands on them, but I'll start by asking Withrow about it and look for hunting equipment when we search his home."

"We need to remember it could also be the

person or persons that Delmar hinted at helping him," Archer offered.

Carothers swung his laser focus back to her. "Any idea who might help Withrow?"

"I honestly don't know very much about Delmar, but from what I do know, I'd guess the most likely person is Stan Fannon. He was engaged to Delmar's sister Cindy and he was at the bridge the day she died. I saw him at an Oregon Free meeting after that and he clearly blames me, too."

"He help plan the bombing?" Archer asked.

She shrugged. "He claimed that he was only there for the peaceful protest and no charges were filed against him. That's why he wasn't kicked out of the Oregon Free group."

"Obviously the group believed him. Do you?"

Did she? "I did, but after seeing how crazy Delmar acted, I just don't know anymore."

Carothers made a note on his pad, then flipped the page. "Tell me everything you know about Fannon."

"The only other thing I know is that he's an electrician and he lives in Troutdale."

"So he's not a local?" Archer asked.

She shook her head.

"Back to these incidents at your B and B," Carothers went on. "Can you think of anything else that happened that can now be attributed to Withrow? Especially something violent with Oregon Free."

She didn't have to think about her answer for very long. "Oregon Free, no, but there were some other incidents at the B and B. They weren't life threatening but…"

Archer came to his feet. "Incidents like what?"

"I don't know where to start."

"Anywhere." He smiled, revealing perfectly straight white teeth, and his already high cheekbones lifted. He was boyishly handsome and her heart flip-flopped, plus she felt a twinge of a smile starting.

Seriously? She'd just gone through a huge trauma and she was tempted to flirt with the guy. Unbelievable.

She directed her answer at Carothers. "The first thing that happened was our website reservation system failed. We didn't realize it at first. We just thought business was slow for a few weeks and then a customer finally called and told us the reservation form didn't work."

"Could just have been a malfunction," Carothers pointed out.

"That's what we thought, too. But the guy we hired to fix it said it had been hacked. I can't provide the specifics as everything he said was tech speak and I really didn't understand it, but

I can give you his contact information and you can get the details from him."

"Did you report the crime?"

She shook her head. "Our repair guy said he doubted it would do any good as the police probably wouldn't be able to track him. We put better security in place to prevent it from occurring again and were just grateful we could take reservations once more."

"What else happened?" Archer asked.

"Our inventory system was hacked, too. The numbers were changed, making it look like we had supplies, but then when we'd go to retrieve them for use, the items were out of stock and we had to buy more expensive goods locally. For the longest time I thought it was because of Birdie's failing memory until it all came to light."

Archer shifted on his feet, widening his stance. "And is that all that happened?"

"No. Someone set up a roadblock on a busy weekend and turned guests away."

"Did you report this incident?" Carothers asked.

She nodded. "We called your office but the deputy was unable to determine who was behind it. In addition to that, we've had deliveries that were mysteriously canceled or didn't show up, and we had an infestation of bedbugs. All of this occurred in the last two months and has taken a serious toll on our business."

"Anything special about the last two months that would make these things start happening?" Carothers probed.

"No clue. And honestly, as I tell you this, I don't believe Delmar would be behind them. He clearly wanted to kill me and none of those things are life threatening."

Following a long pause, Carothers shrugged his shoulders and said, "Maybe he wants to strike back at your aunt, too, by putting her out of business."

"Maybe." She pondered what would have happened to Birdie if Delmar had succeeded in his attempts to kill her and ran the business into the ground. Birdie could sell the property and make out okay, but who would care for her? She would have to be institutionalized.

The thought shattered Emily's heart.

"I really need to get back to the fund-raiser," she said, more determined than ever to make it a success.

"Fine." Carothers handed her a business card. "In case you think of anything that might be helpful."

"I'll walk you to your car," Archer offered in a way that Carothers couldn't refuse.

Emily put the conversation behind her and

went to greet her guests and to assist Birdie's church friends who'd volunteered to work the carnival. At 9:00 p.m., when the crowd had finally thinned, she sat down by the food booth to count the proceeds. She held the metal cash box in her lap and felt her eyes drooping as she waited for Ralph Inman to join her. As the former business manager for the B and B, he'd volunteered to help reconcile the income and receipts for the night.

She saw him working his way through lingering visitors toward her, his hands shoved in baggy pants pockets, his worn leather satchel slung over his shoulder as usual. He wore his typical plaid shirt with a chest pocket. He was short and balding and reminded her of Mr. Magoo. Birdie was a jovial lady by nature and loved to watch old cartoons so Emily could name all of the cartoon characters from years past.

As he approached, he looked at her with the same sharp eye he'd used to keep the B and B's finances in line for the past twenty years, until they'd fallen on hard times. He'd been at Birdie's for so long he was almost part of the family. Thankfully, he'd decided to retire and enjoy life when the business started tanking and they could no longer pay him.

He sat beside her and yawned. "I forgot how much work it takes to run one of these events."

She set the cash box on the table. "Then let's get going on this so we can get you home."

He nodded, flipped pages in his book and they started reviewing the receipts she'd stored in the cash box. She explained each receipt, and he noted them in the expense column in his ledger. He'd never changed over to computerized bookkeeping, which meant Emily would have to add these details in the computerized system she'd created when she started managing the business.

He asked so many detailed questions that the receipts took over thirty minutes to log and then move on to counting the cash.

Ralph rearranged bills so they all faced the same way. "Want me to drop this in the night deposit on my way home?"

"Sure, that'd be great," she replied, but her attention was diverted as she noticed the crowd moving rapidly toward the house. They seemed agitated and upset, which was odd.

"What's going on?" she muttered.

"Fire in the back of the house," a man in their midst called out.

Emily jerked her head around to see flames shooting from a third-floor window. Her bedroom window! Dark smoke billowed from the nearby bedroom.

Birdie.

Emily was vaguely aware of a scream. A wild, air-rending noise.

Had it come from her?

Maybe. She didn't care.

She shoved the cash box at Ralph and ran.

All she cared about was getting inside the house to save Birdie.

FIVE

Archer caught sight of flames greedily licking at an upstairs window, seeking air and fuel to burn brighter.

Emily. Where's Emily?

He shot a look at the food table where he'd seen her just minutes before counting money with Ralph Inman. Ralph sat alone, staring up at the fire.

Archer ran his gaze over the crowd. Caught sight of Emily racing toward the front door of the house.

"Call 911," Archer commanded the woman next to him and took off running.

"Emily, no!" he shouted, but she either didn't hear him or chose not to listen.

He grabbed one of the Bridal Veil T-shirts they were selling, powered toward the house and offered a prayer for help and guidance.

Inside, he paused to listen and assess. The foyer was filled with a light cloud of smoke, but no fire. He heard Emily's footfalls on the stairs to the third floor. She was heading up to the fire. Maybe to Birdie. He started after her, tying the T-shirt over his nose and mouth.

As he climbed, smoke swirled around his body like a living, breathing thing. The color darkened as he climbed higher, and when he hit the top floor, he heard a woman coughing. It didn't take him long to see that the blaze had flared up in Emily's room.

"Emily, call out!" he yelled.

"In here," her voice came from her bedroom.

He ran down the hall and found her trying to lift Birdie from the floor, but she wasn't making any progress. Birdie's breathing was labored and low, but she was conscious. Flames spread across the far wall and smoke billowed from an antique sofa, which Archer suspected was the fire's point of origin.

"Step back," he commanded.

"No, Birdie's my responsibility. I'll do it." Emily started coughing and doubled over as the spasm racked her body.

There was no way she could move Birdie, and yet, she was a fierce protector and wouldn't leave her aunt. He admired this trait, but she would only succeed in killing them both.

His lungs were starting to burn from the smoke, but he ignored the pain and intense desire to get fresh air. He hurried to Emily, moved her out of the way and lifted her aunt into a fire-fighter's hold over his shoulder.

"Go, now!" he shouted at Emily, who was staring up at him, but not moving.

"I…"

He rounded the bed and grabbed her by the wrist, directing her into the hallway. "Pull your shirt up and cover your mouth. Try to stay as low as you can."

As he stepped to the door, water sprinkled from the open window. The fire department couldn't have arrived yet so the people downstairs must have deployed a garden hose.

Please, Lord, let it be enough water to calm this fire.

As they descended the steps, the air became easier to breathe, but his lungs were still raw with pain. His throat was dry, his eyes stinging. Emily kept looking back, slowing them down, and keeping Birdie from needed oxygen. He pushed past Emily and hoped she followed. *If* she had the strength. If she didn't, he'd settle Birdie outside and come back for Emily.

He hit the main level and looked back one last time before racing out the door. Emily's eyes went wide, and she crumpled to the floor. Archer's heart stuttered, and yet, he couldn't help her now.

He burst onto the porch and down the steps, nearly running over a burly man in bib overalls. Archer ripped the T-shirt from his mouth and gulped deep breaths of air.

"What can I do?" the man asked, his focus on Birdie. "I know CPR if that helps."

Archer didn't think twice but handed Birdie over to him. "She's breathing and shouldn't need CPR, but help her any way you can. I'm going back in for Emily."

He charged up the steps to the foyer. Found Emily crawling toward the door. She batted her eyes, and her breathing was labored.

Fear roiled through him as he scooped her up and barreled out the door.

Please, Father, please. Emily. Birdie. Let them both be okay.

Emily continued to battle watery eyes and struggled to breathe. She coughed, then gasped and coughed some more. Despite her pain, he remained optimistic. She hadn't lost consciousness and could breathe on her own. That was a good sign.

"Birdie," Emily finally eked out. "Take me to her. Please…I need to see her."

He thought to argue in case Birdie had taken a turn for the worse, but Emily would fight him off and worsen her own health in the process. He scanned the crowd and saw the man in the overalls kneeling in the grass by the bouncy house where Birdie lay.

"I see her," Archer said and started his way through the crowd.

Emily's coughing fits eased and her breathing improved, but her body remained limp and she made no move to get free.

As the crowd parted, Archer saw another man kneeling next to Birdie, and he seemed to be assessing Birdie's condition. She wore an oxygen mask and Archer followed the line to a mobility cart where an older man sat, his breathing labored.

The man in overalls stood. "Doc's tending to her. Said the oxygen is working and she'll be okay."

Emily squirmed out of his hold and knelt by Birdie, whose eyes were closed.

"Birdie, it's me, Emily. Open your eyes."

Nothing. A guttural sound of pain came from Emily's throat.

How many times in one day did this poor woman have to deal with potential death and loss?

Anger burned in Archer's soul.

It's not fair, Lord. She's suffering. Help her, please.

Birdie's eyes fluttered open, and Emily's shoulders sagged. Archer wanted to follow suit, but he had to stay strong for her and for the crowd. Law enforcement officers were trained to take control and people expected that from them. If he lost his command presence here, people would panic and then he'd have chaos on top of everything else.

Plus, he needed to keep people from trampling a crime scene. Since it appeared as if the fire started in Emily's room, he suspected it was another attack on her life and evidence would be crucial in proving that.

He turned his attention to the building. Two extension ladders leaned against the exterior, both occupied by men spraying water from a hose. Flames no longer framed the window, but plumes of smoke continued to billow into the night sky.

Sirens sounded, but they were still far off in the distance. Archer's first response was relief, but then he saw people blocking the driveway and preventing access to the house.

He turned to the man in overalls. "I need you to station yourself at the house and keep everyone out of the building until the fire department takes over."

"On it," he said and lumbered toward the steps.

Archer turned his attention to the crowd. "Okay, folks, we need to clear the driveway."

He started shooing them back, then once he had the driveway clear he stepped over to Emily. "Are you all right here if I go talk to the fire crew when they arrive?"

"Yes."

She clutched his hand and peered up at him, relief pouring from her dark eyes. "Thank you, Archer. You saved us both again, and I'll never forget it."

Something stirred deep inside him, and he had the sudden desire to lift her in his arms. Hold her close. Just for a moment. Not for her sake, but for his. But the feelings were so foreign he didn't know what it meant so he nodded and said, "Just doing my job."

Her hand fell away, and she took a quick step back, her smile fading. He'd hurt her. How, he had no idea and now wasn't the time to ask. "The medic should be here in a second to tend to you and Birdie."

"I don't need any help." She cleared her throat, belying her statement.

"They'll need to check you out for smoke inhalation."

"I'm fine."

Of course, she'd say that. Miss in control, I can do it all myself and don't need anyone. No wonder she went into accounting. A black-and-white profession. Nothing was gray and muddled. Cash in. Cash out.

He should know. Not about the accounting, but the control part. He did the same thing. He'd come from a wealthy family and had a generous trust fund. People wanted his money, and he couldn't trust anyone's motives. Anyone, except the squad, but even with them, he held back. But unlike Emily, he never claimed to have control. When he went against his parents' wishes for how he lived his life and they'd disowned him, his inability to be in charge of the way they treated him, of everything in his life, became abundantly clear. Emily still fought that battle. Didn't mean she should get her way. Not when it came to her health.

"If you won't let the medics check you out because it's the right thing to do," he said, earning a raise of her eyebrows, "then do it for the medics. They'll have a crazy amount of paperwork to fill out if you decline."

She sighed and clamped her hands on her hips. "Fine. They can give me a checkup. But with this fire, I now have even more to do to keep this place running, so no matter what they say, I won't be going to the ER."

He wasn't even going to try to argue. He admired her strength, but not when she took everything on herself like this. Okay, fine, he was guilty of that, too, but this was different. He didn't want anything from her other than to help her.

Her gaze shifted to the house. "Just our luck to have a fire break out. Probably the old wiring. Or my fan."

Archer had seen the fan in the window and it was still running so he doubted it caused the fire. And old electrical wiring wouldn't spark off the middle of a sofa. "So you think this was an accident, then?"

"You don't?"

He shrugged. Until he was certain of how the blaze started, he wasn't going to share his suspicions and amp up her worry. He was far from an expert on fire and could totally be wrong.

She bit her lip. "It's odd that Birdie was in my bedroom."

The sirens wound nearer and he had to step closer to be heard. "Do you think she could have started the fire?"

Her forehead creased. "Not intentionally, but…yeah…if she was confused at the time, it's entirely possible."

"In the event this wasn't an accident, you should prepare yourself to talk to the fire department's investigator. If he finds something suspicious, a detective will be called in to investigate as well and the first people he'll look at are you and Birdie."

"But why?" She furrowed her brow in confusion. "We wouldn't burn down the B and B. It's our home and we want to see it succeed."

"You do need money."

"To keep the business running, and starting a fire wouldn't accomplish that."

"But they don't know how badly you want to keep Birdie's business afloat," he reminded her. "What they'll see at first is that you could take the insurance money and sell the land, which has got to be worth a pretty penny, then leave all of this behind you."

Emily crossed her arms and planted her feet. "Birdie would never want to leave and I wouldn't risk such a thing. If I was nuts enough to start a fire, I certainly wouldn't do so with Birdie in the bedroom!"

"We both know that, but they don't. So you just be prepared that they will look at the two of you."

She faced the crowd and suddenly spun back. "Ralph. I was with Ralph for…oh…gosh…I don't know. The last hour or so. He can vouch for me."

"Good," Archer replied, but didn't add that an old family friend who might lie for her wasn't an airtight alibi.

The fire truck's light swirled into the darkness near the drive so he reminded Emily to let the medics check her out and then jogged toward the road. The rig bounced over the rutted road and when it reached Archer, he waved the vehicle into the drive, then ran after it.

As soon as the truck came to a stop, a firefighter jumped down and settled a white helmet on his head. Others who streamed out after him wore red helmets, setting the first guy apart and signaling he was in charge of the crew.

Archer saw the captain insignia on the helmet and introduced himself. "The fire started in a third-floor bedroom. Looks like the locals have contained it with hoses."

He frowned. "Bonehead move. Fire can progress rapidly when not controlled properly. This can create unwanted ventilation and greater fire growth or it can result in a backdraft and the building can explode. Then these guys would be in a world of hurt. A building can be replaced but people can't."

Archer totally understood the man's response. If a citizen tried to intervene in police matters, Archer wouldn't appreciate it either. "Anything I can do to help, Captain…?"

"John Parker," he replied quickly. "If you could take up crowd control that would free my men up to do their jobs."

"Sure."

"You'll find yellow tape in the first rig if you need to block off the area."

Archer nodded and stepped to the crowd, who had eased up to the truck for a better view. He ordered them to move back. Most people complied, but of course, there had to be a few guys who wouldn't listen and he had to threaten an arrest before they obeyed his directive.

When he'd gotten everyone out of the way, he let his gaze travel over the crowd until it landed on Emily sitting on the ambulance bumper by Birdie, who lay on a stretcher.

Emily swiveled. Caught him watching her. Her sadness evaporated to be replaced with grim determination. She spoke to Birdie, then stood and crossed the lot toward him.

She stopped in front of him and looked up, her expression blank. "Have you learned anything new?"

"Have you been cleared by the medics?" he fired back.

She nodded.

"Cleared or you refused treatment?" Archer asked.

"Cleared."

"And what about Birdie?"

"Birdie's going to get a bit more oxygen and then we're both good to go." She lifted her chin and dared him to challenge her, but he'd argued with her enough about their health. If they wanted to stay here, and he saw them struggling in the least, he'd ask the team paramedic, Darcie Stevens, to come out and give them a quick checkup.

Emily clenched her hands at her sides and surveyed the area. "I can't just stand around and watch all of this. There must be something I can do to help."

A man stepped into the driveway, giving Archer an idea. "It would be helpful if you wandered through the crowd and took pictures of people. Plus, jotted down the names of as many of them as you know."

"Why?" she asked, crinkling her forehead.

"If this fire was started on purpose, we'll need to interview as many people as possible, but we can't ensure they'll all stick around. A list and pictures will help us find those who go home."

He paused and met her gaze. "Plus, arsonists are known to hang out at fires they've started, and if we're diligent, you could capture the guy on your camera."

SIX

Emily eased through the crowd, snapping pictures and listing the names of the people she recognized. Archer's warning as she'd left him kept sounding in her head. If she spotted Stan Fannon she wasn't to approach him, but head straight back to Archer. So far, she hadn't seen him. She knew most of the people from growing up in Bridal Veil and couldn't believe any of them would be behind the fire. But then, she'd never have believed Delmar would turn into a stark-raving-mad lunatic either.

Fortunately, the heat wave had broken and cool air swept over the crowd, who suddenly swiveled. She followed the direction of their gazes. Captain Parker stepped up to Archer, and she wasn't about to miss their conversation. After all, he could be talking about the fire's origin.

She pushed her way through the onlookers and marched up to the pair.

She was trembling inside from another sense-less tragedy, but she made sure she appeared confident. "Is the fire out?"

Parker's nod was swift as he opened his turn-out coat. "We're in the mopping-up phase now." He faced Archer. "When I arrived, you seemed suspicious of the fire."

Emily opened her mouth to speak, but Archer jumped in before she could say a word and he shared the afternoon's events with Parker.

"If this is a case of arson," he continued, "I suspect friends of Delmar Withrow are behind it."

Emily honestly wasn't ready to admit that someone other than Delmar wanted to kill her so she decided to focus on how the fire started and form her own opinion of what had happened tonight. "Did the fire start in my bedroom?"

Parker nodded, but said nothing more.

She met his gaze to ensure he was listening. "Was it my fan?"

The captain shook his head.

She was getting frustrated at his nonanswers but she wouldn't lose her cool and alienate him. "Then how did it start?"

He eyed her. "I'm not at liberty to say."

"Why in the world not?" she snapped and in-stantly regretted it when he took a step back.

He coolly appraised her, a sour look spreading across his face. "Fires are often started by homeowners who need money and are trying to scam insurance companies. I don't want to inadvertently give you information that could change your story."

This was exactly what Archer had warned her about. Emily opened her mouth to defend herself, then clamped it closed. She *was* in desperate need of money and Parker had likely already gathered that from the fund-raiser.

"Emily was with the former B and B manager, Ralph Inman, for an hour prior to the fire breaking out," Archer offered.

She smiled her thanks, but she could barely lift her lips as after all the stress of the day, fatigue had finally set in.

Parker took off his helmet and swiped a hand over his head. "I'll pass that information on to the investigator when he arrives."

"When will that be?" Emily asked.

"He's en route now." Parker glanced at his watch. "I'd say fifteen minutes or so."

"And if he thinks the fire was deliberately set, then what?" Emily asked.

"Then he'll call in a detective from County. He'll take over and a criminal investigation will be opened."

"In your opinion, was this fire deliberately set?" Emily braced herself for his answer.

"The investigator will tell you more if he can."

She wanted to get to the bottom of this and hated the captain's noncommittal answers. "Can I see my room?"

Parker shook his head. "Official personnel only until the investigator or detective releases the scene. You'll also need to contact your insurance company as they'll most likely want to send out their own investigator."

"But won't your investigator just share his report with my insurance company?"

"Sure he will. We work hand in hand with insurance investigators all the time, as it's often the insurance companies who actually prove arson. They have the money to perform rapid and more thorough tests when our department resources aren't unlimited."

This was getting more complicated and confusing by the minute when all she wanted was to know the cause of the fire and to repair the building so she could resume taking reservations. "Do I have to wait for the insurance investigator before I clean up from the fire?"

"Once the scene has been released to you, that's between you and your insurance company. Any other questions?"

Emily shook her head and so did Archer. Parker settled his helmet back on his head and stepped to his truck.

She sighed in frustration as he walked away. "I just want to know how the fire started. Is that too much to ask?"

Archer stared at her, seeming to weigh something before speaking. Maybe holding something back. Something she needed to know to take control of the situation and move forward?

"What is it?" she demanded.

He scrubbed a hand over his face and took a deep breath. "In my quick peek at the room when I rescued Birdie, it looked like the fire started in your sofa."

"The sofa. That's odd, right? Aren't most fires electrical?"

"I'm not sure about that," Archer said. "But I think the investigator is going to prove that someone started this fire on purpose, and as I told Parker, I think one of Withrow's friends is the most likely culprit."

"You really think they'd go that far?"

"What do you think?"

She ran the day through her mind. The night. The threats. "Stan was devastated when Cindy died, so yeah, he could be that angry. Especially if Delmar riled him up, so I should look into him."

"*We* have to look into him."

Emily quirked a brow. "You want to continue to help me after tonight? Why? What's in it for you?"

"I'm not leaving until I know you're safe."

She peered into blue eyes that were warm and compassionate. He really was one of the good guys, and he gave his help with no ulterior motive other than to be sure she was safe. She shouldn't be surprised as he was a deputy, and law enforcement officers ran toward danger to protect those who ran away.

Runners like her father. Or the men her mother dated. They were all runners.

But Archer?

No, he was a man of his word and she graciously needed to accept his help.

"Thank you." She peered up at him.

He took her hand in his and an irresistibly devastating grin wrinkled the corner of his eyes. All thoughts went out of her head other than wondering what it might be like to kiss him. He captivated her in a way no man ever had, and the warmth of his touch traveled up her arm. His smile suddenly fell and he let go of her hand.

Embarrassed at her reaction, she tucked her hand behind her back. She vowed to be on higher alert with him. Not only to fight her romantic attraction to him. That would be the easy part. But ignoring the nice guy. The man who was proving she could count on him. The man of compassion.

How did she defend herself against that?

By sticking to the business at hand, that's

how. She looked away and spotted local entrepreneur Lance Taylor making a beeline toward her.

"Great," she grumbled. "He's the last person I want to see tonight."

"Who?"

"Lance Taylor." She nodded at him. A runner, he was long and lean, and he had a narrow face with a mean expression. "He's the king of B and Bs in this area, and he keeps trying to buy Birdie's place to add to his holdings. She's told him no a million times, but he refuses to back down."

"You think he might have started this fire so he can ruin the business and get his hands on it?"

"Wouldn't put it past him," she replied, then stopped talking as he was nearing them. If he wanted something, he was relentless and Emily hoped he didn't mention buying the B and B, as she was just too tired and worn down to fight him.

"Evening, Emily," he said, his narrow lips tipping in a forced smile. "Sorry about the fire. Perhaps Birdie will want to sell now."

"Just like you to swoop in on someone's misfortune," Emily snapped.

Lance had turned to look at Archer. "I'm sorry, but I don't think we've met."

Archer introduced himself, but didn't offer his hand in greeting.

"Did you start the fire to get Birdie to sell?" Emily asked before filtering her thoughts.

Lance shook his head. "I'm not a criminal. Just an astute businessman who stopped by to see how your little fund-raiser was doing."

"Awfully convenient for you to be here, then." Archer fixed Lance with a stare that Emily was sure he used on people he caught breaking the law.

Lance ignored Archer and his smile widened. "I guess the event isn't turning out the way you had hoped. Why not end all of this struggling and convince Birdie to sell? I'll pay cash and the two of you can be out of here lounging on some beach somewhere in a matter of days."

Emily planted her hands on her hips and glared up at him. "How many times do we need to tell you that Birdie's isn't for sale before you get it?"

"Things change and I—"

Archer pierced him with an even more direct stare. "She doesn't want to talk to you so back off."

Lance looked at her for a long moment. "If you change your mind you know where to find me." He spun and departed with a flourish, drawing attention as he always did.

Emily blew out her frustration and felt Archer watching her. She'd been so grateful for his help that she'd allowed him to step in on her personal battle with Lance. Normally, she'd tell him he had no business interfering. After all, she'd seen what happened to her mother's life when men butted into it, but she was just too exhausted to deal with additional conflict tonight. If Archer did it again, that was another story, and she'd make sure he understood that she could handle herself.

She looked at him.

"Something about this Taylor guy is hitting me wrong," he said, jaw muscles working. "If your fire was started intentionally, Detective Carothers will want in on this investigation, too. We'll need to make sure to tell him about Taylor."

Just the thought of Carothers coming back out to question her about the fire left her unsettled and told her she needed a break before speaking with him. Birdie needed rest, too.

"If you'll excuse me," Emily said. "I'd like to get Birdie settled in the cottage. Will you let me know what the investigator has to say?"

Archer nodded and Emily crossed to the ambulance. She listened to the medic's instruction for Birdie and then gathered her aunt against her side and escorted her through the crowd and down to the guesthouse.

Emily flipped on the lights and let her gaze linger on the place she'd helped Birdie decorate. The long room made up the entire living area. A large stone fireplace filled one wall, and the other walls were painted white, rising up to a soaring ceiling with dark wooden rafters. The kitchen with a French country design was open to it all. Two bedrooms with a shared bathroom took up the remaining space in the rear of the building.

Birdie wandered into the space and ran her fingers over decorations that she had lovingly picked just after Emily's sixteenth birthday. Now she stared at them with vacant eyes and a troubled look.

"You remember the cottage, right?" Emily asked.

"No," she said matter-of-factly. Birdie had slipped back into her fog, but at least she wasn't agitated, which leaving the B and B often caused.

Her aunt stepped to the bedrooms and gave them a long study before planting her feet outside the last door. "This isn't right. I want my room."

Emily would rather have her own room, too, but she didn't need a sense of familiarity the way Birdie did. "I'm sorry, Birdie, but the power is out in the main house, and we can't possibly stay there tonight."

Emily didn't add that they couldn't even enter the house because of the arson possibility. And, of course, with the big hole in the roof, they wouldn't be sleeping in their own beds for some time. If they ever did again. She had no idea if the emergency fund that she'd managed to hold on to would cover the repair costs.

"I was afraid." Birdie grabbed one of the robes they provided in guest baskets and rubbed it over her cheek. "I woke up and couldn't see. Tried to get out. Then I got lost in the room. You helped me. Thank you."

She spoke the words as if Emily was a stranger, not a beloved niece. The fact was, in this moment, Emily *was* a stranger. The thought cut her to the core and she was torn between falling to a heap on the floor in tears or hugging Birdie in an effort to comfort her. Neither solved anything. Birdie would stiffen up and grow agitated. Crumbling to the floor would bother her aunt even more.

Truth be told, Emily most likely wanted the hug for herself. It had been a horrible day and she just wanted to be held until it all went away. The story of her life, and she'd get through this the same way she'd gotten through so many things. With resolve and control.

She went to the window. Stared up at the house. Saw Archer stroll across the lawn with the investigator.

She remembered Archer's smile, and instead of letting it go, she allowed her mind to wander over what it would feel like to have his strong arms circle around her right now. To rest her head on his broad chest. Feel his heartbeat and know security, a feeling that had been missing since Birdie started her decline.

For a moment you'd feel safe, but then what?

Then memories of the men her mother had chosen in haste would come flooding back and she'd pull away from Archer before she started to care for the guy. Okay, fine, she'd already started caring. Not even a full day together and she had to admit she liked him.

It's just the trauma speaking, she told herself.

How could she not have fond feelings for the man who rescued her twice in one day? And yet, he was practically a stranger so how could she even think she knew him let alone care about him?

She supposed she'd have to be a coldhearted woman not to feel something, and she was far from that. Though, men she'd met and who had tried to ask her out over the years would likely say she was. But she'd simply spent years developing the ability to hide her true feelings from others.

She let the curtain fall and turned back to Birdie, but she was missing. Emily's heart hitched and she swung her gaze to the front door. It remained closed so she went to the first bedroom, where she found Birdie had climbed beneath the covers and was already fast asleep.

Emily tried hard not to worry about this brave woman who meant so much to her, but it lingered every day. Birdie had been declining fast and lately she'd been sleeping a lot. Emily didn't know if that was natural or not. If it continued, she would call the doctor. But for tonight, she was just relieved her aunt was safe and sound.

Emily retrieved a bottle of water that they kept stocked in the refrigerator for their guests and made a mental note to talk to Archer about getting food supplies from the main house for morning breakfast.

Taking it to the sofa, she dug out her phone and the crumpled list holding names of people attending the fund-raiser. She started through the pictures she'd snapped. When she discovered an unfamiliar face, she jotted down the number of the photo for further research.

Every time a noise sounded from outside she sat up and waited for Archer to arrive with news from the investigator, but she finished reviewing the pictures and he still hadn't shown up.

She went to the door to check on the progress outside. A crew of firefighters were securing the roof with a bright blue tarp and wooden slats. Their rhythmic pounding sounded like giant woodpeckers. Another crew was placing large fans by the doors, drawing out the smoke. The harsh scent clung to the air and memories of finding Birdie came rushing back.

What if Archer hadn't been able to save Birdie?

A bolt of terror shot through Emily.

Hard as it was to admit, she needed Archer here. Needed him badly, as the charred building without a roof told her Delmar's words were coming true. This wasn't over.

SEVEN

After three long hours spent with Detective Carothers and the fire investigator, Archer took weary steps to the cottage front door. He found the main room lit with a single lamp in the corner, but no sign of Emily or Birdie. He shifted his gaze to two doorways on the far wall, both of them open. A night-light glowed from one, the other was dark. Bedrooms, he supposed.

Archer suspected Birdie slept in the room with the light in case she woke up confused. He stepped closer to the doors, but he stopped short of actually looking into the rooms and invading their privacy.

"Emily," he whispered, hoping she was asleep and he wouldn't have to give her more bad news tonight.

He heard movement, and she soon entered the living room. Her hair was damp and she wore stretchy black pants, paired with a blue-and-red-striped top with a large white sweater that swallowed her hands. She smelled of lavender instead of the caustic smoke still clinging to his clothes. Dark circles lingered under her eyes, and she rubbed them, then blinked a few times.

"Sorry if I woke you," he said softly.

"I wasn't asleep," she replied. "You have news?"

"Let's sit down."

"Sitting down means the news isn't good," she said, but still dropped onto the sofa, looking expectantly up at him.

Just like a death notification call, it was best to come right out with the news to erase all lingering hope and help the person to accept their loss, but man, he hated to do it. "The fire was started by someone pouring gasoline onto the sofa in your room."

"Are they sure?" she asked, her tone flat.

He didn't expect her calm reaction, but maybe she was too worn out to conjure up any emotion. He took a seat on the coffee table in front of her and resisted the urge to reach out and lace his fingers with hers. "They found a gas can in the room and you can still smell the fuel on the fabric."

"Then it's official. Someone wanted to burn down the B and B." She wrapped her arms around her stomach. "Now we just have to figure out who."

If she was thinking ahead, then she was taking this better than he expected.

"Did they find any evidence that might help us locate the arsonist?" she asked.

"Carothers will have forensics process the gas can for fingerprints and also try to track down the store where the can was purchased. He was focusing on Stan Fannon, but after I told him about Lance Taylor, Carothers added him to his list, too."

She furrowed her brow. "I get how the prints will help, but not the purchase part."

"If it's an item sold exclusively at one store, and they have security cameras, we can request the video to get a look at all the people who recently bought the can," he explained. "But you should know, it may not work as the arsonist could have owned the can for a long time."

"Is that likely?"

He nodded. "The investigator said he was sure it wasn't a professional arsonist. So yeah, it could be a can that the arsonist had lying around his house."

"Not that I expected this to be started by a professional, but how can they rule it out so easily?"

"You know where the wall behind your bed is open and you can see the wood structure?"

She nodded. "A pipe burst a few weeks back

and they had to cut open the wall to fix it. I hated not finishing the repair, but with our money situation, I couldn't justify it." She uncrossed her arms and leaned back on the sofa. "So what does that have to do with the fire?"

"The area adjacent to a flammable wall is the best point to initiate a fire. The supporting wood is exposed, making it the most flammable wall in the room. If the fire had been started there, flames would have quickly caught on the wood and spread through the house. Plus your bedding would have been excellent tinder. A skilled arsonist would know that."

"But the sofa has fabric, too. Wouldn't it be just as combustible?" She tried to cross her legs but Archer was in the way.

He scooted back. "That's what I asked, but apparently antique sofas stuffed with horsehair and covered with wool fabrics like yours are difficult to ignite and don't burn readily once started."

"Interesting," she said and sat thinking. "So this means pretty much anyone could have started the fire, except honestly, I can't see Lance getting his hands dirty."

"He could have hired someone to do it for him."

"I suppose," she conceded. "Thankfully I have an alibi or I could see where they might suspect me."

He didn't respond.

"What are you not telling me?"

"You're not in the clear yet," he answered in a low tone. "Carothers is still investigating your ties to Withrow and hasn't had time to confirm that you weren't part of the attack this afternoon."

She took a frustrated breath and blew it out. "I get that he has to keep looking into me even though it's a colossal waste of time, but the fire? I have an alibi. Ralph—"

"Remember, Ralph is an old family friend and until recently he's had a vested interest in the business."

"Ralph's as honest as they come." She sat forward and rested her elbows on her knees. "He wouldn't lie to the police."

"Still, Carothers is a good detective and he'll do his due diligence. He'll ask others who might have seen you and Ralph together to confirm the alibi. Only then will he release the house back to you."

"Again, a waste of time when the real arsonist is getting away with it." She got up and started pacing.

The real arsonist. Archer used his phone to connect to the internet and research Stan Fannon while he waited for the investigator to do his thing. Archer confirmed he lived in Troutdale and was a self-employed electrician as Emily had mentioned. The guy had a couple of misdemeanors on his record, but Archer could find nothing else that would indicate he was serious trouble.

Didn't mean anything, though. Most person-on-person crimes were fueled by emotions and when something hit a person wrong, even decent folks who had no criminal background could snap. Cindy's death could be such a catalyst in Stan's life, which means he was still Archer's main suspect.

"When you scanned the crowd, did you see Stan or anyone else that Withrow had hung out with in the past?" Archer asked.

Emily shook her head and continued to pace. "He wasn't the least bit friendly with other members of Oregon Free. Of course, I don't know the people he might hang out with outside the group, if anyone."

Archer stood and crossed to the window, where she stared into the distance. He could almost see the wheels turning in her head.

She suddenly blinked hard, then stared up at him. "Did they let you inside the house to assess the damage?"

"No. Carothers won't let anyone set foot inside until after the forensic team finishes their work."

"When will that be?"

"Hard to say. They're on scene now and Carothers will let me know when we can have access."

A tiny frown line appeared between her brows as she absently tapped her finger on the windowsill. "I've managed to keep a small emergency fund. Hopefully it will be enough."

He wanted to tell her everything would turn out fine, but he didn't know that it would.

She closed her eyes tightly and started taking deep breaths. "I can get through this. All I need is a solid plan. We have guests registered for the day after tomorrow. If I can get the roofer and electrician started the minute Carothers turns over the house, we should be good to go."

Archer bit down on his tongue before he said that there was no way anyone would want to stay in a place that reeked of smoke, but she would come to that conclusion all on her own once she saw the building in the light of day.

He met her gaze squarely. "I'll pray that you succeed."

She shot him a confused look. "Prayers? Oh, yeah. Right. Thanks."

Her less than enthusiastic response surprised him. "After seeing Birdie's church friends helping with the fund-raiser tonight I assumed you were a woman of faith, too."

"I am. It's just…at the moment…" She shrugged.

"I don't think prayers are doing much good in my life. Since I moved back here, all I'm getting from God is silence." She took a deep breath. "But maybe it's different for you. Maybe He answers your prayers."

"I trust that God will provide answers even if it isn't the answer I want to hear."

She raised an eyebrow at his vague answer and watched him carefully. "So you're saying that my prayers aren't going unanswered, God is just saying no to my requests."

"Maybe, or the answer could be yes, but not now. It will occur in God's way and in His timing."

She sighed, drawing it out for a long moment. "I don't have time and God knows that. Our finances are so dire that if I don't get this place repaired in time for our guests, I might as well forget making the repairs and put the padlock on the door now."

The next morning, Archer steeled his resolve and approached Stan Fannon. Emily seemed as if she wanted to hang back, but Archer wasn't surprised by that. He wouldn't be eager to see someone who was angry with him either. It would be even worse with a guy who potentially wanted to kill him.

Fannon had his head down and was running wire through a conduit outside a Troutdale post office. He wore jeans, mud-caked hiking boots and a faded T-shirt with a picture of a popular rock band across his skinny chest. His head came up, and he looked to be in his thirties with just the beginning of crow's feet by eyes filled with defiance and anger. The guy might have only a few misdemeanors on his record, but Archer took an instant dislike to him.

"We have a few questions for you," Archer said.

Fannon slowly came to his feet and tugged up his jeans. "Why would I want to talk to either of you?"

Archer wasn't on duty, which meant he couldn't flash a badge, so he pulled back his shoulders, making sure the FRS logo was visible on his chest.

"It would be better to answer my questions here than to be hauled in for questioning," he said, though he had no official status in this investigation.

"Fine."

Archer wanted to lead by asking about bow hunting, but records from the Department of Fish and Wildlife hadn't come in yet, and if it turned out that Fannon was a hunter, Archer didn't want to tip the guy off so he ditched any equipment he might own.

That left the fire for Archer to focus on. "Where were you last night?"

Fannon eyed him for a moment, then shrugged. "I worked here all day. Finished up about five. Grabbed a burger on the way home and watched TV all night."

"Alone?"

"Yeah, I'm alone all the time now thanks to her." He jerked his thumb at Emily.

She opened her mouth and Archer suspected she was going to say Cindy's accident wasn't her fault, but he preempted her by asking, "What did you watch?"

Fannon didn't answer for a moment and Archer suspected a lie was coming. "*American Chopper* marathon."

"What network is that show on?"

"Discovery Channel."

Archer tapped the screen on his phone and brought up the Discovery Channel's TV listings for last night.

"Funny thing," he said, holding out the phone. "The show wasn't on last night."

Fannon crossed his arms over his chest. "Maybe the schedule for my cable company is different."

"Maybe," Archer said, though he doubted it. "What company do you use?"

"Oregon Cable."

"Great." Archer stowed his phone. "I'll just give them a call today to confirm you were watching it."

"They can't tell you what I was watching."

"You have a DVR?" Archer asked.

"Yeah, sure."

"Well, guess what?" he went on in a matter-of-fact tone. "DVRs are computers that track all sorts of data about your watching habits, and your cable company can tell me what show you were tuned in to and for how long." Archer didn't add that it would take a warrant to get that information and they had no probable cause to request one. "Of course, that doesn't prove you were in the room watching, now, does it?"

Fannon didn't say anything, but his nostrils flared and he spun toward Emily. "We wouldn't even be having this conversation if it wasn't for you."

She fisted her hands. "Cindy's death was an accident."

"Don't bother trying to defend yourself. Cindy's death is all your fault and nothing you say is going to change my opinion of you." His eyes flashed with anger as he raised his index finger and advanced on Emily.

She stood strong, as if waiting for him to come closer.

Archer wasn't about to let that happen so he stepped between them and pinned Fannon with a look. "I'd back away if I were you."

Fannon ran his gaze over Archer, as if the guy thought he could take him. Archer widened his stance and fixed the same stare on Fannon that Archer used on uncooperative arrestees.

"You are not allowed to lay a finger on Emily. Not here. Not anywhere." Archer jabbed the guy in the chest exactly as the jerk had planned to do to Emily. "You got it?"

"Yeah. I got it." His focus traveled back to Emily. "You may think you're going to get away with this but you're not, you know."

Archer raised his eyebrow and folded his arms over his chest. "Is that a threat?"

"Take it however you want," he replied, a snide smile slithering across his mouth.

This conversation was going nowhere fast...in fact, Emily's presence was inciting the guy and that would not end well. It was best they leave.

"Remember my warning," Archer called over his shoulder as he escorted Emily to the car.

Unfortunately, the questioning had not gone the way Archer had planned. He not only still didn't have a clue whether Fannon had a valid alibi, but he feared the conversation had made an enemy of the man and could cause him to escalate any plans he might have to harm Emily.

EIGHT

Archer's anger at Stan radiated off his body as they walked. Emily was fighting to control her temper, too, and as an added bonus, she was also upset with Archer. She wouldn't have allowed Stan to hurt her and Archer's repeated interference irritated her last nerve. She'd seen her mom roll over and let guys take over her life in just the same way. Take over Emily's life while they were at it, too. She would not allow that.

Archer's hand went directly to her car door, but she jerked it open herself, earning a questioning look. He stood confused for a few moments, then stepped around the front of the car and settled behind the wheel. He looked like he wanted to say something but instead shoved the keys in the ignition.

She took a few deep breaths to try to calm her irritation, then said, "I can fight my own battles, you know."

His eyes scrunched up in confusion again

and he peered at her for several long moments. "What are you talking about?"

"Your coming to my rescue with Stan back there. With Lance last night. Neither of them would have hurt me, and I can handle myself in situations like that. I've done it for years, and I didn't need your help."

"Did you want him touching you?" Archer's eyes bore into hers. "If so, tell me, and if it happens again, I'll back off."

She met his gaze head-on. "I don't want him or any man touching me...but I decide that. Not you."

He pulled back as if she'd slapped him and held up his hands. "Message received."

Emily sighed. She hadn't meant to hurt him and wished she'd have taken time to cool down so she didn't come on so strong. "Look, I'm sorry. I didn't mean to offend you. Especially not after everything you've done and are doing for me and Birdie. It's just..." She shrugged. "Guys thinking they know what's best for me and taking over...it's one of my pet peeves."

He continued to stare at her, and she'd have to be blind not to see he wanted an explanation. She didn't particularly want to give it, but after his kindness and all the time he was devoting to her, he deserved to hear her reasoning.

"It's my dad," she said and looked away. "He

took off when I was a little kid. My mom didn't think she should be alone so it seemed like every time I turned around she had a new boyfriend. The constant in our house was the parade of guys going through it. Most of them didn't respect my boundaries and thought they could fill in for my dad when I wanted nothing to do with them."

She looked at him again. "But why give them a chance when I knew they wouldn't be around very long? So, you see, I have a thing about guys stepping in for me when I can handle myself. I had to learn how to do it at a very young age, and by the time I came to live with Birdie, I'd had to grow up and fend for myself."

"So what you're saying is to butt out of your business." His jaw firmed for a moment and some unreadable emotion flashed in his eyes before he ground his teeth. "You want me to take off? Just say the word, and I'm out of here."

"No, please. That's not what I meant at all. I'm grateful for your protection—"

"But you don't think you need it?"

"No, I do, it's just…" She sighed. "I don't know. Maybe it's more. You…me…there's something going on between us, right? And I don't want you to think just because you're stepping in to protect me that it's going anywhere."

He let his gaze linger. "So you feel it, too?"

"That's not the point."

"Isn't it?"

He had her there, but she wouldn't acknowledge it. She glanced away again and felt his gaze on her, but she wouldn't turn back. He was right. It *was* the point. She didn't mind his taking Stan down a notch. In fact, she actually liked having someone on her side. Someone willing to defend her. And as she'd said, that was the problem. She couldn't, no *wouldn't*, start to rely on someone, just for the person to turn around and bail on her.

She met his gaze and firmed her own. "I appreciate your willingness to protect us, but I'd also understand if you want to take off. I'll do my best to keep us safe on my own. I always have."

"If you want my protection, then you'll have it, but please don't let your emotions get the best of you and take these threats lightly. They're very real and you need to be extremely careful."

Birdie slept in late the following morning, and Emily took advantage of the time to check out the damage at the B and B. Archer trailed behind, and for once, she wasn't aware of him except for the reassuring sound of his footfalls as she surveyed the first floor. Carothers had called Archer late last night to release the building to her. She'd wanted to rush over and inspect it, but Archer was the voice of reason. He said seeing the damage would be easier in the light of day.

He was wrong. Daylight or not, it wasn't easier to accept that someone would go to such extreme lengths to be rid of her.

The lingering stench of smoke seeped from the walls, the floors, and it was so strong she questioned if the first two floors had actually been spared from the flames. She stepped into the living room, where the heavy velvet drapes really reeked of smoke. Likely permeated all upholstered furniture and perhaps her precious books, as well.

She moved on to the dining room. The smell seemed stronger there, but fortunately no damage.

"Other than the smoke," Archer said, "it's looking good on this floor."

"I'll still need to figure out how to get the smell out, but you're right. No damage so far. Not even water damage."

The sun slipped behind heavy clouds, suddenly extinguishing the sun's bright rays filtering through the window and darkening the room, leaving shadows and an ominous feeling hanging in the air. She'd brought a flashlight for the upstairs hallway, and with the electricity still out, she clicked it on to step into the kitchen.

Thankfully, it had sustained no damage, lifting a bit of the heaviness in her heart. The upstairs would be another story.

Emily preceded Archer up the back stairway. As soon as she hit the landing the *plop, plop, plop* of water caught her attention. She swung the flashlight up to see large drops falling from the ceiling at the end of the hallway. Not surprising, as this section was located below the third-floor staff quarters.

Although she'd expected to see this, her heart still sank. She steeled her mind before looking at the other end of the hall.

Perfectly dry.

The situation was bad, but not dire. In fact, something they should be able to recover from.

"This doesn't look bad at all," Archer said in a gentle voice. "You said God's been silent, but seems like He was watching out for you here."

Had God spared them?

"He could have prevented the fire altogether," she replied and the minute the statement left her mouth, she knew it was a surly response that should have been left unsaid.

"But He has a purpose for it and the damage could have been far more extensive."

Archer was right. She'd been looking at all the trials that had come into her life as do-or-die situations, when she needed to start seeing the gray areas. Areas such as Archer's rescues yesterday and last night that had allowed them to escape unscathed. "I suppose you have a point... I need to remember what I have to be thankful for even when bad things keep happening."

She moved on to the guest bedrooms and found most of them habitable. "I'll have to get the floors dried out and get rid of the smoke smell, but we should be open again soon."

"You're not still planning on taking guests tomorrow, are you?"

"If I work hard today and the electrician has good news for me, I might be able to get this place ready on time."

He quirked a brow. "Are you sure you're up to that?"

"Up to it?" She pondered his question. "Hard work could be just the thing to keep my mind off the threats." She swung her flashlight toward the third-floor stairway. "This is the part I really dread seeing."

With each step, her last climb up the stairs last night came rushing back.

The smoke. The darkness. The fear that Birdie hadn't made it.

Emily swallowed hard and stepped into her bedroom. Her eyes went to a charred path starting at the sofa and running up the wall. From there, flames traveled into the ceiling and burned clear through the roof, revealing the blue tarp the firefighters had affixed outside.

She could almost see the flames. Feel them. See Birdie lying deathly still on the floor. Emily's heart had nearly failed when she'd stepped into the room. Dear, sweet Birdie in trouble because Emily had come back to Bridal Veil. But again, as Archer pointed out, it could have been worse.

A new thought sent a shudder through her and a chill seeped into her bones. "What if Birdie had run into the arsonist? I could have lost her."

"But you didn't." Archer moved up behind her and settled his big hands on her shoulders.

The warmth traveled through her body, chasing out the chill and searing her like the flames that had torched this room. She should pull away, but she liked his touch. Liked the comfort.

Ha! Imagine that. She'd recently told Archer she didn't want any man to touch her. Now she didn't want to break away.

During a sleepless night thinking about him as he slept on the sofa in the other room, she'd decided that she was getting too attached to him, and she promised herself that she would keep her distance today.

Now here she was. Not even nine o'clock and her mind had traveled to how much she was starting to like having him around. Even more, she was starting to think she could trust him, but her emotions were a jumbled mess right now, and she wasn't sure if she was seeing clearly. It felt so similar to her mother saying yes to yet another man who wasn't right for her.

Emily stepped away. "I should get going. I have a lot to do to get ready for my guests."

She left the room, vowing to shake off her developing feelings for Archer before she let them blind her into doing something stupid, or worse yet, forget she was fighting for her life.

NINE

Despite Archer's protests, Emily had insisted on cooking a hearty breakfast for him and Birdie before they began their day. He'd offered to help with the meal, but she refused. Something was up with her this morning. The change started upstairs in her room. Continued as they ate. Her warm, caring nature was present only for Birdie, who seemed stuck in her early years when Emily came to live at the B and B.

Emily occasionally looked at him, but her expression was blank and reserved. Only when he'd rested his hands on her shoulders in her room did she relax for a moment. She even seemed to like his touch. Until she suddenly didn't and slipped away, not willing to look at him.

He sipped on his piping-hot cup of coffee, his mind wandering, his gaze landing on her as she finished eating scrambled eggs.

Might as well put the padlock on the door now.

Her words from the night of the fire continued to rumble through his head. He couldn't get rid of them. Not when he had the means to step in and help her but was choosing not to do so.

His large trust fund sat untouched, and he could easily give her the money to make her needed repairs. For that matter, he could give her enough money to ensure the business never failed.

Not like he was using the money. At least not much of it for himself. He did his best to live on his deputy's salary, but he had to admit that sometimes his income didn't stretch to some of the nicer things he'd grown accustomed to having. So from time to time, he dipped into the fund, but he didn't even come close to spending the interest on his account. He gave a lot of the money to charities every year and considered forming his own nonprofit organization, but he hadn't settled on a cause yet.

"I'm stuffed," Emily said as she pushed away her plate and looked up.

He forced himself to meet her gaze. She diverted her eyes, but not before a little smile flitted across her lips.

She really was acting odd this morning. Was it because, despite her good intentions, her interest in him was growing, and like him, she didn't want to feel anything?

Or…worse, had she Googled him, discovered he was loaded and now she was putting on this shy act to try to snare him?

He just didn't know. Couldn't know. Never could with women.

She got up to grab the coffeepot. He set down his cup and she filled it, standing well away from him as if touching him was like getting the plague.

She was such an enigma. A strong, confident, some would say stubborn woman, but then she could give him a smile so sweet and innocent that it made his heart ache. A personality in direct opposition to the gold diggers once circling his world.

He curled his fingers around the warm cup and his thoughts turned to wondering what it would it be like to have breakfast with her on a regular basis.

He wanted to believe she wasn't the kind of woman who cared only about money. Not like the women he'd once dated. But she desperately needed an infusion of cash, and she would do just about anything to save the business. Not for herself. No, it was a selfless act for her aunt, like most of her actions, but even more reason to pretend to care for him to get her hands on his cash.

Maybe he should just give the money to her and be done with it. Then he'd know he could never trust her feelings toward him, and he could quit stressing about it. It would be simple. A bank transfer was all it would take. A few clicks of a mouse and keyboard, and she'd have the funds to save the B and B.

Right. Do it.

With that single little click, he'd lose all hope of ever getting to know the real Emily Graves. For her to get to know the real him. Could he abide by that decision?

A loud knock sounded on the door, startling Birdie and Emily. Archer came to his feet, coffee sloshing over the rim of his cup.

Emily shot him a look. "Maybe it's Carothers."

"He'd call first." Archer headed for the door, still holding his mug. "Hopefully, it's the reinforcements I arranged."

She raised a questioning gaze to him. "The what?"

He met her eyes. "You'll see in a minute, but in case I'm wrong, wait here until I give the all-clear."

From the small window beside the door, he confirmed his suspicions. Most of the FRS team and their significant others stood on the porch holding construction tools and supplies.

"It's okay, Emily," he called out and unlocked the door.

She joined him, her footfalls hesitant, her gaze apprehensive. "I don't like surprises."

"Don't worry. It's a good one." Archer pulled open the door and hoped she wouldn't think something was wrong because standing before her were the very people who rescued her from Withrow.

Jake held up a hammer, a broad smile on his face. "Point us to the work."

"What?" Emily shot a look at Archer. "Why's your team here?"

"To help fix the roof and clean the place up for your guests." He stepped outside and clamped his hands on Cash Dixon's shoulders. "This is Cash. He's our bomb expert. But don't worry, his job today is to help secure your roof, not blow it up."

Cash wrapped an arm around his wife's shoulders. "My wife, Krista, isn't so good with a hammer, but I hear the house will need cleaning, and man, I never understood the meaning of *clean* before I married her."

She jokingly elbowed him and smiled at Emily. "Doesn't take much to be neater and cleaner than Cash."

Darcie stepped forward, her hand in Noah's.

"In case you don't remember me, I'm Darcie and this is my fiancé, Noah Lockhart."

Noah shook hands with Emily. "Glad to be here."

"No Skyler or Brady?" Archer asked.

"Skyler's too wrapped up in a homicide to come during the day," Darcie said, then looked at Emily. "And Brady pulled an eleven-hour shift. He and his fiancée, Morgan, plus Skyler and her hubby, Logan, will join us tonight if we're still here."

"Are *all* the members of your team married or engaged?" she joked, but Archer could see something was troubling her. Maybe it was just the surprise visit but he detected something else, too.

"Jake and I have managed to avoid the net." Archer laughed as he always did when this subject had come up in the past, but today he didn't feel good about his response and wanted to give Emily a straight answer.

Maybe he should have, as his joke fell flat and an awkward moment ended the lighthearted exchange.

"Okay, so enough with the introductions." Jake shoved a tote bag into Archer's hands. "The clothes and things you asked for."

"Yeah, man." Cash smiled. "You better get changed, Archer. Your shirt has a wrinkle in it."

"I've been in the truck with this clown for over an hour." Jake rolled his eyes and raised his hammer. "Point me in the direction of something where I can pound out my frustration."

Archer looked at Cash's pickup filled with plywood and roofing materials. "Go ahead and pull the truck around the east side of the B and B, and we'll get started on the roof."

"Wait." The word exploded from Emily's mouth, stilling everyone. She stared up at Archer, the earlier uneasiness weighing heavy in her eyes. "You should have asked about this first."

"If you're worried about our qualifications to repair a roof, don't be," Jake said. "My foster dad was a contractor and I worked construction jobs with him for years. I could replace a roof in my sleep. Now, if we find structural damage you'll want to hire a contractor, but we can handle a simple roof replacement."

"It's not that." She bit her lip. "I don't know if or when I can pay for these materials."

Darcie offered one of the comforting smiles that she was known for and laid a hand on Emily's arm. "No need to pay. They've been donated."

"By who?" Suspicion darkened Emily's tone.

Darcie's smile faltered and she dropped her hand. "A woman named Winnie Kerr. She's a good friend who loves to help out when needed."

"She donated the old firehouse we all live in," Archer added so Emily didn't feel singled out. "She had it remodeled just for our team. We each have our own condo, and she continues to pay all the bills."

Emily narrowed her eyes and crossed her arms as she seemed to weigh her answer carefully. "I don't take charity. I'll pay her back."

Interesting response. What might she have said if Archer had offered to lend her the money?

Darcie waved a hand. "Feel free to pay her back if you want, but she doesn't expect it."

"So are we working or what?" Cash asked, sounding grumpy.

"Don't mind him." Krista rolled her eyes. "He didn't get enough coffee this morning."

"I'll be happy to make a pot."

Archer held up his cup. "She makes good coffee."

Emily flushed at the compliment and Darcie fixed a questioning look on Emily.

Archer loved Darcie like a sister and never wanted to hurt her feelings, but she'd clearly spotted the uneasy vibe between him and Emily. And that meant Darcie would be a royal pest today and he'd have to take her aside and tell her to stand down before she embarrassed him or Emily.

Emily suddenly took a step back, likely from

Darcie's intensity. "Before I start the coffee, has anyone heard about the shooting victim who is still in critical condition?"

"I checked on him this morning," Darcie said. "He came through surgery just fine and is in ICU."

"I'm glad to hear he made it through the surgery," Emily said, but looked like an animal trapped in a car's headlights. Not surprising. All eyes were on her and the team could seem intense to an outsider. Archer had even cringed under their scrutiny when he first joined the group.

"We should get to work," he said to draw their gazes.

Emily nodded. "I'll go put that pot on."

Darcie held out her medical bag. "Archer wanted me to check on you and Birdie so I'm coming with you."

Emily shot Archer a desperate look, then stepped toward the door.

"Remember, Emily," he called after her, "if you leave the house, you need to stay within eyesight at all times."

She nodded but kept going.

Darcie spun to face him. "Something going on between the two of you?"

"No." Archer wouldn't discuss his developing

feelings with Darcie and certainly not in front of the whole group. "Come on, let's get started."

He led the team to the charred side of the house, and Archer had to admit the place looked far worse in the light of day. Cash pulled up his pickup, and they started unloading ladders and equipment. Archer hadn't seen the inside of a gym for two days now and could get behind a morning of solid backbreaking work. Sure, he still put Emily's safety front and center, but what better place than a view from the roof to make sure no one snuck onto her property.

He leaned a ladder on the side of the house and extended it to the full length.

Once he reached the top, he surveyed the property for any threat. The sky was clear, the sun warm, and birds chirped in the trees. The area was free from danger. Blessedly free for once. But Archer was still antsy. He was used to a schedule. Things planned at certain times. Since he'd been with Emily, his time had been solely dictated by leads they located, and that left him unsettled.

Another ladder came to rest next to him and footsteps sounded on the rungs.

Jake soon reached the top. "Know what you're looking at?"

"A roof with a tarp on it," Archer joked.

Jake huffed a short laugh. "I meant the repairs. Any idea where to start?"

"I'm guessing we remove the shingles."

"Wrong." Jake's expression sobered. "First we make sure the rafters aren't compromised and it's safe for the team to walk up here."

"Right. Safety. Your number one thing."

"I know you all get tired of hearing it, but we have a perfect track record and I wouldn't want to ruin it in our off hours."

Archer couldn't argue with Jake's logic or his concern for his team.

"I'll check it out," Jake said. "Then we'll get started on those shingles. A flat shovel works best to scrape them off so I suggest you grab one."

Archer nodded and started down the ladder. At the bottom, he searched for gloves in a bin just as Emily stepped across the grass with a checked tablecloth across her arm. Darcie followed with a large tray holding a pot of coffee and a large tin.

Emily unfurled the fabric and it settled over a long picnic table painted white. She attached little clamps to the corners, then Darcie set down the tray.

Emily opened the white tin and faced them. "I made muffins yesterday morning so they're still reasonably fresh, and I just ground the beans for the coffee. So enjoy."

"You didn't have to do all of this," Krista said, putting down a large carton of nails she'd unloaded from the truck.

Emily waved off the comment. "It's the least I can do."

Archer watched as Krista joined Emily and Darcie. The trio soon started chatting like old friends. A cool breeze played over the area, rustling wisps of hair around Emily's face. She'd changed into an old plaid shirt and holey jeans likely in preparation for the nasty job of cleaning up the house. As much as he was a neat freak, he loved seeing her rumpled. Somehow, it made the setting so real and homey, not fake like when his family gathered for lawn parties in the home they rented each summer, everyone wearing the latest designer fashions.

He'd felt out of place there, but here—in a foreign environment—he surprisingly felt at peace. Contented. He'd spent enough time away from servants, maids and workers hired to do just about everything to see that by being raised in the lap of luxury he'd missed out on personal connections.

Connections he continued to be hard-pressed to make due to his money. He'd often thought he should give it all away, but couldn't bring himself to do so. It was his safety net in case he failed at the new life he was carving out for himself. He jerked on the gloves, grabbed a shovel, then climbed the ladder.

"Good news." Jake stepped across the roof toward him. "They contained the fire in time to leave the support structure intact. Just the sheathing and shingles need replacing so we're good to go."

Jake waved him up. "Start with scraping the shingles free and tossing them to the ground. Be careful not to take anyone out when you do."

Archer set to work, putting his frustration into his arms and clearing a large section in a matter of minutes.

"Whoa," Jake said. "Slow down or you'll burn out."

Archer leaned on the end of his shovel. "Guess I'm trying to work out my frustrations. I don't like not knowing who's lurking out there. Did Carothers share any updates with you?"

"He questioned Withrow at the jail, but the guy won't talk. Carothers also requested the bow-hunting information and pulled the incident report for when the arrow was fired at Emily. There was nothing you wouldn't expect in the report."

"Can I get a copy of it anyway?" Archer

hoped when he got a look at it that he would find a lead of some sort.

"I'll email it to you."

"What about forensics? Anything there?"

"No prints on the gas can, but the good news is that it's a proprietary item from one of the big auto parts stores," Jake replied, flicking a glance his way. "It's a newer item sold only in the last few months so Carothers is working on getting video footage for customers who purchased that model."

"Could be a lot of footage to go through."

"Depends on how long the stores keep their video files. Also, you should know that the cans are sold online. Carothers is requesting sales information for those transactions, too." Jake's eyes narrowed. "Did you turn up anything new in the pictures Emily took the night of the fire?"

Archer shook his head. "We passed the pics and Emily's list on to Carothers. He has a team interviewing everyone on the list, but there're fifty or more names on there."

"It'll take weeks to get through all of them." Jake propped a hand over his eyes to block the sun as he stared over Archer's shoulder. "That doesn't look good."

"What?" Archer asked.

Jake pointed across the lot. A lime-green sedan drove up and parked at the road a quarter mile from Emily's driveway. A man climbed out of the driver's seat. He leaned on the roof of the vehicle, lifted a pair of binoculars and peered at the house.

Archer's brain fired on all circuits and his innate sense of danger put his senses on high alert. The guy tossed the binoculars into the car and started up the driveway. He walked in a halting, limping gait and seemed to be filled with purpose. Archer shot a concerned look at Emily. She was sitting at the picnic table with the other women. Right in the guy's intended path.

He wouldn't try to hurt Emily in front of them all, would he? Withrow hadn't minded an audience, in fact, he craved one.

Archer's adrenaline surged. No way he would let the man get close to her. He dropped the shovel and charged for the ladder.

"Slow down," Jake warned. "Remember. Safety first."

"I'm thinking about safety," Archer muttered. "Emily's safety."

TEN

Emily got up from the picnic table. She would have liked to continue talking with Darcie and Krista, but she had a lot to accomplish while Birdie napped. In addition to cleaning up from the fire, several loads of laundry waited for her. There were eggs to collect, a garden to water and produce to harvest.

"Emily!" Archer shouted from his ladder. He was descending so fast she suspected the house might be on fire again. He hit the ground and charged in her direction.

She glanced at Jake, who held his hand over his eyes and stared at the road. Was there another problem? Another imminent attack?

Her heart started racing and she faced Archer again.

"In the house. Now!" His authoritative voice rang through the clearing as he rushed to her side and directed her toward the door. "There's a guy on his way up the drive. He was watching the house."

"Cash," Jake yelled. "Check the guy out."

She heard movement behind her, but didn't slow down to confirm Cash was on the move. She hurried up the steps and inside the house where Archer locked the door after them. She went straight to the big picture window in the living room to see what was occurring outside.

Archer joined her and jerked the curtains closed. "Stay away from the window."

She stared at him. "Aren't you overreacting?"

He lifted his gaze to her face. Worry hung in his eyes. "This guy could be a threat."

"Do you really think this guy is going to try to hurt me with you all here?"

"I suspect it's not every day that a man sits in his car at the road and watches your house with binoculars."

His statement brought back similar incidents that had occurred in the past few months. "Not every day, but it has happened. Did you get a good look at this man and can you describe him?"

"Short, bald, pudgy."

"Lime-green car?" she queried.

"Yes, you know him?"

She nodded. "Freddie Baumann. He's a disgruntled guest who stayed here six months ago.

He was injured when he fell through a rotten floorboard on the third floor."

Archer raised a brow. "What was he doing in your personal living area?"

Emily hated to tell this story, as she'd had to recount it so many times, and even ended up testifying in civil court when Freddie sued them for his injury. But if Archer was going to continue to help them, he needed to know about the situation.

She took a deep breath and blew it out before starting. "The injury occurred before I moved back here. I was visiting for the weekend, and Freddie nagged me to go out with him. I kept saying no, but he wouldn't give up. On his last day here, he snuck upstairs hoping to find me."

"Persistent guy." A crease appeared between Archer's brows. "Not that I'm surprised. I can understand why a guy would go to extreme lengths to get your attention."

"You can?"

Archer held her gaze for a long moment, and she was unable to look away. "Of course. You're beautiful. Generous and caring. Why wouldn't a guy want to date you?"

"Maybe because I try my best to give a hands-off vibe to all men." She crossed her arms for emphasis.

"So that's what's going on here." He gestured

between them. "It's not just me you're pushing away, it's *all* men."

"Most guys get my signals." She gave him a pointed look. "Some, like Freddie, don't and I need to verbally tell them to back off."

A flash of irritation darkened his eyes. She'd hit a nerve. Good. Maybe he'd ease up on the interest he was transmitting, and she wouldn't have to work so hard to keep her guard up around him.

He parted the curtains and peered out before turning back. "Looks like Cash has everything under control. He intercepted Freddie and is talking to him."

"I really don't think Freddie's a threat. He's angry, yes. And hates me? Totally. But kill me? I doubt it."

"So let's sit down and you can tell me about him." Archer gestured at the sofa.

Emily perched on the edge of a club chair instead to prevent him from sitting close enough so she could catch a whiff of the minty soap from his morning shower.

He leaned against the wall, his pose meant to appear casual, she supposed, but his gaze was razor sharp, and his hand rested on his sidearm.

"Like I said," she stated, "Freddie followed me upstairs and waited in the hallway for me to come out of my room. When I did, he hurried toward me. There were several rotten floorboards that we hadn't gotten around to fixing so I yelled at him to stop. He ignored me like he'd been doing for days and kept coming. The wood cracked, and he fell through."

The frustration of the day came flooding back, and she released a shaky breath. "He asked me to help him free his leg. I recommended we wait for professional assistance, but he kept harping at me until I finally complied. I shouldn't have. I knew better. And when the jagged wood ripped his leg open, I was mortified. He ended up being hospitalized, where he developed a staph infection, and they wound up amputating his leg."

"They say people often get sicker in a hospital than when they went in."

"I know, right?" She swallowed past the emotion clogging her throat. "But he blamed me for the loss of his leg. And maybe he was right, I don't know. If I'd waited for help, he wouldn't have been injured."

Archer pushed off the wall and planted his feet. "But he badgered you to help."

"Still, that's not how he told his side of the story, and it was his word against mine when he sued us."

"That's not fair."

"Maybe not, but I *had* suggested we wait for professional help to extract him and then went against my own plan of action. His lawyers brought that up in court. Made me look like an idiot for trying to help him." Sighing, she clasped her hands tightly in her lap. "But the real kicker was that he claimed we were negligent in maintaining the building."

"But he was trespassing in an area where guests didn't belong," Archer argued.

"Our attorney tried using that in our defense, but the judge claimed that the burden of guests' safety fell on our shoulders. If we didn't want our customers in the private quarters then we should have secured the area."

"I can see his point but still…" He lifted a shoulder in the briefest of shrugs.

"The good news for us is that Freddie didn't go to a follow-up doctor's appointment so the judge claimed he was negligent in not seeking appropriate medical care on a timely basis, too. As a result, he got very little money. The bad news is that our insurance rates skyrocketed and the attorney bills…" She shook her head. "Those bills are what started the financial downfall of the B and B, and the reason I put all of my savings into the business, then came back here to try to revive it."

A contemplative look crossed Archer's face. "So why does Freddie sit at the road and watch you?"

"He's mad. Simple as that. He was a roofer but with his leg issue he can't work anymore so he sits there glaring up at the place instead. Seems to make him happy. If we pass by, he curses us and goes into a tirade. It's like he wants to do something to get back at us, but he's trying to figure out what to do."

Archer chewed on the inside of his cheek for a moment. "You said you once thought the pot rack and arrow were accidents, but the other things that occurred—didn't you wonder if Freddie could be behind them?"

"Honestly, no. In hindsight, I guess I should have questioned it, but the computer repair guy said many businesses get hacked, and I thought the computer issues were just a run of bad luck. And if I *had* questioned it, as a roofer, I wouldn't think Freddie possessed computer skills."

"Do you think he's capable of starting a fire?"

"Capable?" Emily considered it. "I don't know. I mean anyone can start a fire, right? And if he's mad enough, I suppose he might choose that route to get back at us."

A gleam appeared in Archer's eyes and he angled a look her way. "Think back to the days when you saw Freddie. Did any of the strange events or even the attempts on your life happen on those days?"

"I don't know. Maybe."

"Can you pin down the days Freddie visited?"

She caught sight of the B and B calendar sitting on the sign-in table in the foyer. "I can look at our calendar of events to see if I can figure it out." She hurried to the foyer to grab it.

Archer came after her. "You're too close to the window." He put his hand on her back and urged her toward the living room.

His touch gave Emily a sense of comfort—of well-being—but at the same time, it worried her. She thought telling him about Freddie would ease Archer's concern and he'd stand down a bit, but his hypervigilant expression stayed in place, leaving her just as uneasy.

She returned to the chair and ran her finger over the reservations and events to see if she could reconstruct her days. Furrowing her brow, she spotted Mrs. Wicker's reservation. She was the sweetest bird-watcher who'd spent a week at the B and B. Emily smiled as she remembered how famously the woman got along with Birdie. Mrs. Wicker had a ready laugh and was short and stout because she loved her desserts. Particularly cheesecake.

Cheesecake. Emily's heart skipped a beat.

"Here." She jabbed her finger on the last Saturday of Mrs. Wicker's visit. "The day the pot rack fell. Freddie was here. I didn't see him, but I remember because I was in the middle of making a cheesecake for Mrs. Wicker that day. She'd gone to a bird-watching meeting, and when she returned, she told me about Freddie's car at the road."

"Then Baumann should definitely be added to our suspect list. He's as viable as Taylor or Fannon."

Emily shot a glance his way. "But Delmar already admitted he did it."

"He also denied it, so we can't take his word for anything," he reminded her.

"Then how did he know about it?"

"News travels fast in small towns. He could have heard about it and simply mentioned it at the standoff to scare you." Archer started for the foyer, his hand firmly planted on his sidearm.

"Where are you going?"

"To talk to Baumann," he got out between clenched teeth.

"Sounds like you're going to do more than talk."

He eyed her. "Let me be clear about this, Emily. I don't like what the guy did to you. Dragging you through court for something he did. Don't like it one bit. But all I plan to do is ask him a few questions. Now, if during that time, he tries something…" The side of Archer's mouth curved up. "That will be a different matter."

He stepped to the door. "You stay here and away from the windows. I'll have Noah stand duty on the front porch."

"Noah, really? Don't tell me he's a deputy, too."

"We're not *all* deputies, you know."

"I didn't think you could be."

"He's a Portland police detective." Archer winked and stepped outside.

Despite his warnings, she went to the window and watched. After speaking with Noah, he marched straight to Freddie. Archer held his shoulders in a hard line and he fisted his hands at his side.

She'd never met a man like him. One who put others first. Her father was a taker. Everything was all about him. And the other guys her mother had ended up with? All takers, too. Her mother seemed to attract the type. Emily had had the same problem in the past, making it easy to stay detached.

Until now. Until Archer.

He seemed genuine. Not hiding some big secret that would blow up a relationship. Not living only for himself. When he decided to settle down, he'd make some woman very happy. It just wouldn't be her.

She continued to watch him talk to Freddie. Nearly thirty minutes passed when Freddie raised a fist as if to punch Archer, but suddenly let his hand fall and limped down the driveway with Cash as his escort.

When Freddie was out of view, Archer jogged back to the house. He mumbled something to Noah, then stepped inside and joined her in the living room.

She returned to her chair. "What did Freddie have to say?"

"Not much. He was belligerent about most everything. I had no authority to pressure him and he knew it. He claimed he'd heard about the fire in passing and came by just to see if everyone was okay."

"Right, like he cares about us," she said. "And he lives in Portland so I doubt he heard about the fire in passing."

"My thoughts exactly."

"Doesn't mean he started the fire, though." She couldn't believe she was defending Freddie.

"You're right, but when I asked him where he was that night, he just smiled."

Sighing in frustration, she slid him a look. "So what happens next?"

"I'll call Carothers and make sure he brings

Baumann in for questioning. If he's guilty, hopefully he'll lose his bravado under interrogation and confess."

The door opened and Cash marched inside. "Baumann's on his way, but you should know, I saw ammo clips in his car."

Archer's eyes widened. "You think he's carrying?"

Cash nodded. "I had no right to search his car or even ask for his permit, but man, you gotta think he's carrying. Otherwise, why would he have ammo in his car?"

"No reason," Archer said, concern oozing through his words. "No reason at all."

In the cottage, Emily grabbed fresh fruit draining in the colander and arranged it on a platter to round out the lunch she'd prepared for Birdie and the team. The men kept working on the roof and the women used a shop vac connected to a generator they'd brought from Portland to remove water upstairs and prepare the guest rooms. Emily helped them for a while, but then spent the rest of the morning with Birdie and their electrician. The fire hadn't damaged any of the electrical lines and they'd been cleared to use the power again.

Emily put the platter on her tray. She half expected Krista or Darcie to offer to help set the table. That's the kind of women she'd discovered they were. Emily didn't need to give them a task. They just pitched in wherever needed. And Emily would like to call them friends. But she was rusty in the making-friends department. Rusty, ha! She was just plain out of her league.

So many times over the years her mother moved in or married a guy. Not really caring that meant Emily moved, too. New schools. Upended at a whim. Meant Emily had very few friends. As an adult, she was socially awkward much of the time. But these women? This group? They were proving easy to get to know. How amazing that they gave up their day to help her out. Then there was Archer's kindness in arranging it all.

She heard shovels scraping on the roof. Saw through the window, the shingles tossed to the ground. Archer worked so hard on her behalf. If it had been up to her to find local volunteers to do the work, she would have gone to Birdie's church family for help. Emily was always welcome at that church even if she hadn't attended much since she'd come back. But asking for help? She'd feel like she was taking advantage of them. The same with the Oregon Free group. She tried to make meetings and assist in the causes, but she had to stay with Birdie most of the time. So she took on keeping their books. A solitary activity.

She glanced at the team members outside and sighed.

Her life was empty. Not only since she moved back here, but in Portland, too. She just never took the risk of getting to know someone only to be hurt by them. The story of her life.

Shaking her head, she carried the fruit to the dining table. She'd planned to serve the meal to her guests for lunch, but when she called to tell them about the construction work, they canceled their reservation. Frankly, she couldn't stomach another cancellation so she asked if they'd like to stay in the cottage for free and they agreed. They'd arrive later that day when Jake said the roof would be completed. She and Birdie would move into guest rooms at the B and B, and Krista had offered to clean the cottage.

Emily took one last look at the table, then deciding it was ready and filled with enough food to feed these hungry workers, she stepped outside. Thankfully, the expected high temperature would be a seasonable seventy-five degrees today and a gentle breeze drifted across the yard as she joined the group.

"Lunch is ready," she called out.

Cash dropped a bundle of shingles back onto the bed of his truck and jerked off his gloves, then stuffed them in his pocket. "Don't have to tell me twice."

He crossed over to Krista, took the shovel out of her hands and stepped toward the porch.

Krista held up dirt-covered hands. "Where can we wash up?"

"The kitchen or bathroom is fine." Emily stood back and watched as the rest of the team took their time. She glanced at Cash who was already stepping inside the cottage with his arm around Krista.

"Cash might be in a hurry to eat, but you should see Brady." Darcie grinned. "Mention food and he's quicker than a bullet."

"And Archer?" Emily asked as he hadn't come down from the roof yet.

"He's not quick to act, but when he does, he's decisive." Darcie stared at Emily for long, uncomfortable moments. "He's a good guy, if that's what you're asking. Can be quiet and reserved, but he has a heart of gold and any woman would be lucky to have him."

Darcie mirrored Emily's thoughts to a T. "I'm sure they would."

"But not you?"

"I'm not in the market for a relationship."

"Because?" Darcie asked directly.

Emily had to force her mouth not to drop open

at Darcie's prying question. "You don't pull any punches, do you?"

"I did. For years. Hid behind my own issues like you seem to be doing. But you know what I learned?"

"What?" Emily asked as she really was curious to hear the answer.

"Are you a woman of faith?"

Emily nodded.

"Then all I need to say is let go of whatever you're worrying about. Choosing a life of worry when peace is available is foolish. You'll only drown in the worry and miss the best God has waiting for you."

Drown in worry. Yeah, she was drowning all right, but God could also stop the problems, thus ending her worry, right? Or simply give her a hint that He was there, listening.

Are You there, Father? Can You hear me?

"Uh-oh." Archer came up behind Darcie, putting an abrupt end to Emily's thoughts. "Looks like you two are far too serious. Anything I can do to help?"

"Yeah," Darcie said. "Follow your feelings for once in your life and forget about the money."

"Money?" Emily asked in confusion.

"It's nothing worth discussing." Archer tightened his jaw. "Didn't you hear? Lunch is ready."

Darcie raised an eyebrow, but said nothing and started for the cottage.

They all settled at the table with plates filled with fruit, homegrown veggies and thick roast beef sandwiches, but Darcie's comment about money kept plaguing Emily and she didn't feel like eating.

Could Archer be in dire financial straits like she and Birdie were? If so, she totally understood and wouldn't judge him, but she wouldn't ask him about it either and risk embarrassing him. She'd wait to see if he brought it up.

Krista suddenly groaned. "These tomatoes are to die for. Are they from your garden?"

Emily nodded. "It's an heirloom variety that I grow every year. These are the first ripe ones from the vine."

"Skyler's really into gardening, too," Darcie shared. "You should talk to her about it next time you see her."

Emily didn't miss Darcie's point that she expected, in addition to seeing Skyler at the mall shooting, there would be a "next time" that they'd meet. Emily doubted that would occur unless it involved finding the person trying to kill her.

"While you're all here," Archer cut in as if preempting anything else Darcie might say, "Emily, why don't you share the incidents that have occurred in the past and we can get the team members' take on them."

Glad for the distraction from the money comment, she explained the strange incidents. "Delmar seems to want to take credit for the attempts on my life."

"I know you guys have been looking into Withrow's friend Stan," Cash said. "Any thoughts on his other friends?"

She shook her head. "I never really saw him interact with anyone else at the Oregon Free meetings."

"Is that one of your groups at school?" Birdie asked, still locked in Emily's teen years.

"No," Emily answered and didn't expound on Birdie's mistaken time frame, as it would just add to her confusion.

"When is the next scheduled meeting?" Jake asked.

"It's held the first Wednesday of the month."

"Tonight, then." Archer frowned.

"I'm sure they'll be talking about the shooting," Emily added. "It would be great to be there in case they shared something that could help."

"One of us could go," Cash offered.

"No offense, Cash," she said, "but a lot of the members don't trust or respect cops and you would get nowhere with them. I'll try to find someone to stay with Birdie and I can go."

"No!" Archer's vehement response drew the attention of his friends. He took a breath and let it out slowly.

"I don't want you going out of the house at night," he added, his voice gentler. "If the person behind these attacks is a member of the group, it could be dangerous."

"If it *is* one of the group members," Jake said, meeting Archer's gaze, "they'll likely take the night off to attend the meeting."

Archer jutted out his chin. "And if it's not them? Remember…we're still looking at Taylor and Baumann, too."

"I'm sure after that outburst you wouldn't let Emily go without you, so she'll be fine." Darcie faced Emily. "Noah can catch a ride home with the team, and I'll be glad to stay with Birdie so you can go."

"Darcie," Archer warned.

Emily was glad for his concern, but she would go to the meeting. She smiled at Darcie. "Thank you. I appreciate your staying with Birdie."

"Stay with me?" Birdie looked up from spearing a piece of cantaloupe. "Why do you need to stay with me?"

Darcie smiled gently. "It's always nice to have company, isn't it?"

Birdie nodded and looked at Emily. "You have some lovely friends, Emily."

"Okay, it's settled, then." Darcie winked at Emily. "You will be going to the Oregon Free meeting tonight."

Cash glanced at Archer. "If members have an issue with law enforcement, then you're gonna stick out like a sore thumb at that meeting, and they're bound to clam up."

"Emily's not going alone." Archer's voice was razor sharp. "She can do all the talking. I'll hang in the background and observe."

Emily shot him a look. "You can't outright question or accuse anyone of wrongdoing."

"No problem." A lopsided smile crossed his mouth. "I *am* a negotiator after all and have active listening skills."

"Better yet." A mischievous glint appeared in Darcie's eyes. "Why don't you pretend to be Emily's boyfriend from Portland? The members are sure to be more accepting of that."

"Darcie," Noah warned. "Don't start meddling."

"I'm only offering a good alternative." She pretended to pout. "Of course, I'm not a sworn deputy like the rest of you, so maybe my ideas aren't any good."

"No," Jake said. "It's a great idea." He focused on Archer. "What do you think, buddy? You up for being Emily's boyfriend for a night?"

Archer gave a clipped nod of agreement, but Emily would be lying if she didn't admit she was hurt by the reluctance she saw in his eyes.

ELEVEN

The Oregon Free members met in the small back room of a local burger restaurant that evening. Archer escorted Emily inside, and his muscles ached in spots where he didn't know he had muscles. He worked out on a regular basis, but after a day of carrying sixty-pound bundles of shingles up a ladder, he now knew the true meaning of backbreaking work.

Emily set a large basket of vegetables from her garden and cartons of eggs on a table already laden with similar items. Apparently, they swapped homegrown and homemade items. She greeted her fellow members and received mixed responses. Initially, she introduced him as her friend, but when that elicited strange looks, he stepped up next to her and draped his arm around her shoulder to make their supposed relationship clearer.

Knowing looks passed around the room and despite his finely pressed khakis and button-down shirt, so unlike the well-worn jeans and T-shirts on most of the guys, they seemed to accept him. A friendly banter flowed between the members as they exchanged items. Emily finally seemed to relax, but he remained alert. He kept his arm firmly around her shoulder and his eye on the entire group, covertly scoping out signs of concealed weapons, but was gratified not to find any hint of one.

As they took their seats, one of the guys brought up the shooting. Archer felt Emily stiffen beneath his arm. He squeezed to let her know he was there for her and received a sweet smile for his efforts.

"It must have been horrible, Emily," a woman with frizzy brown hair commiserated. "How on earth did you survive?"

"It wasn't easy." Emily took a seat and her closed expression didn't encourage discussion.

If she were a trained law enforcement officer, she would have taken the opening and run with it instead of discouraging conversation. Archer's gut reaction was to step in, but he restrained himself because he knew his interference this early on would put them off.

"I figured Delmar was trouble," the woman went on. "We probably should have voted to remove Stan from the group, too."

"Why's that?" Emily asked casually, and

Archer wanted to give her an atta-girl for her open-ended question that would keep this conversation going.

"I suspect he knew all about Delmar's plan to bomb the bridge and was on board with it. If Cindy hadn't intervened...poor Cindy." The woman shook her head. "Poor, poor Cindy. She was such a sweet girl, not like Delmar at all, and she didn't deserve to die."

"Do you think Delmar let anyone else in on the plan?" Emily asked.

"Delmar? Nah. He was a loner, right?" The woman queried the rest of the group with a questioning gaze.

A young man with a stocking cap not fully hiding his greasy hair nodded. "I think the only reason Stan hung with Delmar was because of Cindy."

"Then why would he go along with Withrow's plan?" Archer asked and all the members turned to stare at him with *What's it to you?* looks.

"I'm just curious," he quickly added.

"I don't really know much about Stan," the young guy said, then looked at his group. "Anyone else?"

"All I know is he lives in Troutdale and used to come to the meetings with Cindy," the curly-haired woman replied. "He kept to himself, and he seemed kind of mean or maybe just standoffish. I don't know which. We haven't seen him except for that one meeting right after Cindy died." She cast a knowing look at Emily.

"You mean the night when he cursed me out," Emily replied, sounding strong and in control.

Archer was so proud of her bravado. He squeezed her hand under the table.

"Yeah, that's the one I meant," the woman said. "I don't want to sound mean, but I think it's good that he hasn't come back or we might have to consider kicking him out, too."

"Do any of you think he might still be planning to carry out Withrow's plan?" Archer asked.

"The bomb at the bridge you mean?" the young guy asked.

Archer nodded and let his gaze wander the group to measure their response. Some nodded and others shrugged, but not a one of them shook their head, further cementing Fallon as the kind of man who would engage in violence, which made him a prime suspect on Archer's list.

"Time to get started, people." An older man with gray hair pulled back into a ponytail and threadbare but clean clothing stepped to the head of the table and the members swiveled to face him.

Emily sighed out a long breath, and Archer

squeezed her hand again to show his support, then he held it for the rest of the meeting. She likely thought he was trying to maintain their undercover status, but in reality, she was vulnerable in this room of people he didn't know or hadn't vetted. Even if they all did seem like an easygoing, peaceful group.

They talked passionately about saving the environment, and he grew antsy. He honestly didn't think about the environment very often. Sure, he recycled, but he didn't live off the land the way many of these people did. In fact, he didn't live a very sustainable lifestyle at all. He'd grown up in a world of luxury that was all about consumerism. Discarding things that were in perfectly good condition to buy the latest fad. He didn't live that way anymore, but after listening to the group, he vowed to evaluate how he could lessen his carbon footprint even more.

When the meeting broke up, the leader approached Emily.

"Something you should know," he said, his tone dire. "After that last meeting when Stan went off on you…"

"Yes?" The word came out on a breath.

"Well, a few of us went out with him for a drink. Stan had quite a few. He said he was going to get even."

"Did he say how?" Archer asked.

"Nah, he didn't even really say with who or what for."

"But you assumed he meant me," Emily said in slow, measured tones.

"Yeah…yeah. I mean we'd been talking about Delmar. So yeah. Had to mean you." He looked at other members walking out of the building. "None of us condone what Delmar did, you know. There's a better way."

"I agree," she said. "I appreciate your telling me."

"No problem." He shoved his hands in his pockets. "I'd want to know if a guy was gunning for me."

Emily's shoulders came up in a hard line. She was understandably upset. So was he, but he wasn't going to let it stand in the way of watching out for her.

"C'mon," he said, reaching for her hand and lacing her fingers through his. "Let's get you out of here."

"Why?" She shot a look around the area. "You think Stan is hanging in the bushes waiting to attack?"

"It's a very good possibility," he said, catching her by surprise. He didn't let her dwell on it, but he whisked her across the lot and safely into this car.

Once they were on the road, he let out a relieved breath and took a read on Emily's mood. She sat rigid and unspeaking, staring out the window.

He should get her talking about something to forget Fannon. "How did you get involved in environmental issues?"

"Meaning what's a numbers nerd like me doing with a group like this?" She chuckled.

"First, I don't find you to be any kind of nerd, and second, even if you like numbers—" he mocked a shudder "—you can still like the environment."

"I take it you don't care for accounting."

"Actually, I have an MBA."

She swiveled to face him. "Seriously?"

"Seriously. Did it for my dad, but I hated business. Everything about it. Especially sitting behind a desk all day. So I decided to find something exciting where I could help people. And voilà, I'm a deputy."

She tapped her finger on her chin for a moment. "Okay, so you don't like sitting behind a desk, and it seems as if you don't like the outdoors much. What *do* you like?"

"I'm still figuring that out."

"Well, if you'd like to experience more of the outdoors, once this is all over, I'd be glad to be your tour guide."

Was she joking? He glanced at her to see, but

the dash lights cast a red glow on her face, revealing a serious expression. How about that? Seemed like she still wanted to know him after they apprehended their suspect.

His heart lifted. For a moment. Until he turned onto the B and B driveway and slammed on his brakes. One side of the large B and B sign that usually hung over the driveway had given way and was dangling across the drive.

"Accident?" she asked as she stared out the window.

"Doubtful." Archer leaned across her to reach the glove compartment for his flashlight. "Wait here while I check."

He got out and strode to the sign, where he ran the beam over the top of the pole and inspected both of the large eyebolts that held the sign in place. He lowered his light and made a closer inspection of the end of the sign lying in the dirt. Shaking his head, he stood and pocketed his light, then lifted the sign and dragged it out of their way.

He climbed back into the car. "The bolt was cut. Would take a power tool, a ladder and some time to do this."

"Darcie and Birdie. Do you think they're okay?"

"Only one way to find out." He put his SUV into gear and sped down the driveway.

The sky was jet black, the moon hiding behind clouds and raising Archer's anxiety. Shadows clung to the large house. A single porch light cast a weak glow, doing nothing to expose danger that could be lurking anywhere.

"Wait here," he said and charged for the front door. He alternated his gaze between the door and the car as he knocked on the door.

Darcie soon answered and she confirmed everything was okay inside. He jogged back down the stairs. Instead of stopping to tell Emily what Darcie had said, he settled his flashlight's beam on the shrubs at the base of the porch, followed by a check of both sides of the home. He spun and at the sight of the vast property lying before him, he sighed in frustration. The place was too big to assess danger lurking in the distance, leaving Emily vulnerable.

He opened her door and connected with her troubled gaze. "Darcie and Birdie are fine. They didn't hear a thing. Everything looks all right, but to be sure, we'll go straight to the house."

She gave a clipped nod and exited the car. He wrapped an arm around her waist and pulled her close. She didn't struggle to free herself, but matched her strides to his. Inside, she tried to move away, but he kept hold of her and spun to lock the dead bolt. Darcie was nowhere in sight so he lingered with Emily at his side and peered into her eyes wide with concern. He hated seeing the fear once again lodged on her face. Hated seeing anything other than the sweet smile he occasionally caught.

"You know I probably overreacted by holding you so close on the way in, right?" he said, putting humor in his tone.

"You're just saying that because you want me to relax."

"You can see right through me, can't you?" Amazing. He'd been raised to keep his emotions hidden. Either she was very astute or he was losing his touch. "You're the first person who's been able to read me that well."

"You've never known anyone like me, then." Her voice was breathless, her eyes locked on his.

The air in the room suddenly was supercharged and warm. He turned a fraction. Touched her cheek. She smiled. Not the soft and sweet one he'd come to know, but a smile with promise. Her cocoa-brown eyes were liquid and questioning, but he had no answers. Even if he did, when she looked at him that way, he could barely think.

"You guys ever—" Darcie said from the doorway. "Oh, sorry. Didn't mean to interrupt…"

Emily spun out of his hold and ran a hand over her hair, as if thinking smoothing it out would make the moment less awkward for all of them. "How'd it go with Birdie?"

Darcie watched her for a moment, and Archer hoped she would answer Emily's question and not start quizzing them about what was going on between them.

"She slept a lot of the time," Darcie finally said. "Is that normal for Birdie?"

"I don't know about normal, but it's become common this last week." Emily twisted her hands together. "I thought I'd talk to her doctor if it continued."

Darcie nodded her agreement. "You take such good care of her."

"She's been like a mother to me, and she's all I have. I'll go check on her." Emily left the room without so much as a backward glance at Archer.

He turned to Darcie. "Before you go, I wanted to ask if you'd be available to sit with Birdie after your shifts until we catch whoever's threatening Emily."

"So you can do a little more cuddling with Emily?" Darcie considered him with an unwavering gaze.

"No," he said, more firmly than needed. "So she can take a break. She has so much on her plate right now. Dealing with the Alzheimer's is hard enough, but the shooting, the fire and Freddie. She's a strong woman, but if she doesn't get some relief, I'm afraid she might crack."

"That's very thoughtful of you," Darcie said.

"Thoughtful or not, it's the right thing to do."

She dug her phone from her pocket and flipped through her calendar. "I have a morning shift tomorrow and Isabel will be in school, but I'll have to coordinate with Pilar to see if she's free to watch Isabel on other days."

Archer hated taking time away from Isabel. Darcie was in the process of adopting the six-year-old girl who Darcie had helped rescue on a callout. But right now, he didn't see any other option.

"And, of course, I'll want to check with Noah," Darcie added.

"Of course." It'd been a long time since he'd had to think about someone else before committing to doing something and he sometimes forgot that others had to do so. "I'm heading out to do my perimeter check so I'll walk you to the door."

She gathered her things and by the time she turned, her expression had become serious. "You can't run forever, you know. Don't ignore what's staring you in face. After all, it's what you're really searching for. I should know. I fought it with the best of them before I surrendered."

On the porch, he paused to get his focus in

the right place. Darcie was hinting at love. He had no time for that or even room for thinking about it. He couldn't afford any kind of distraction. Distractions could end disastrously.

"Let me know when you're available," he said, ending the conversation.

She frowned at him, but then said good-night and climbed into her car.

After she drove off, he jogged down the steps and called Carothers to bring forensics in yet one more time to process the bolt. Hopefully they could match it to the tool used to cut it. A kind of tool that he suspected Fallon might own.

Archer kept the house in his periphery, his light bouncing ahead as he made a grid-like search of the property. He found himself needing to refocus each time his mind wandered to their interaction in the foyer. He was attracted to Emily, no doubt. What guy wouldn't be? But it went beyond her looks. To her as a person. She stirred a part of his heart and soul that had never been touched before. Truth was, he'd let his fear of being taken advantage of stop him from feeling anything.

Question was, what did he plan to do about it…if anything?

Blowing out a frustrated breath, he climbed the steps, and once back inside, he twisted the lock and took a minute to find a positive mood so he didn't add to Emily's burdens.

"Everything okay?" she called from the sofa in the family room.

He nodded, but checked the lock one more time. "Darcie's headed home. What about Birdie? Is she doing okay?"

Emily grinned. "Can't you hear her snoring?"

Archer cocked an ear toward the stairwell and when he picked up the sound of rhythmic snores, he grinned and his mood lightened for real.

He joined Emily, taking a seat in a club chair across from her. "FYI, I asked Darcie to come by tomorrow to sit with Birdie and give you a bit of a break."

Irritation flared in her eyes. "You did what?"

"I thought you needed some relief from the stress of everything that's been happening coupled with caring for Birdie."

She didn't speak and he could feel tension rolling off her. "You're mad at me for interfering again."

"Mad? No."

"But upset."

She shrugged, but her annoyance remained lodged in her eyes.

"Okay, I get it. I should have asked you before talking to Darcie, but maybe deep down, I thought you'd say no, and you need a break."

"I would have."

"But why? Darcie is excellent with people and you could use the rest."

She cast an appraising look his way, but he hadn't a clue what she was trying to ascertain.

"What is it?" he asked.

She clenched her hands together and got up to pace. "You're taking over again. It reminds me of my mom when she brought a new guy home. She'd given them a kiss and cuddle and suddenly they thought they could take over and rule our lives. And she let them." She stared at him for a long moment, burning a hole through him. "You can't imagine what it's like to have your life upended time after time. The rules changed all the time. To forget the current guy's new rules and then be punished when you failed to keep them."

He had no idea this issue ran so deep. He stood. Stepped over to her. She backed away.

"I'm sorry," he said, injecting sincerity into his voice. "I didn't mean to tread on a sore spot."

"Well, you did." Her tone held a definite edge that he hadn't heard before. "I've got things covered. I can take care of Birdie and myself just fine."

Archer had to bite his tongue not to mention how her life was falling apart around her and she wasn't doing fine at all. He'd said enough already.

She was right.

He had no business messing with her personal life. Probably no business being here at all, and yet, there was no way he was walking away while someone wanted her dead.

TWELVE

Where am I?

Emily blinked her lashes hard, searching to figure out her location. She saw a familiar ginger jar lamp and white side table. A quilted bedspread on the unmade bed. A hint of smoke in the air.

A guest room. Birdie! She's missing.

Emily shot to her feet. She was worried that her aunt might have a bad night in the strange room so Emily had sat by her bed in the glider and had fallen asleep. Somehow Birdie had left the room without waking Emily. Meant Birdie likely recognized where she was or she probably would have panicked. Emily had to make sure her aunt was okay.

She headed into the hallway, and at the top of the stairs, she heard voices in the living room.

Archer and Birdie.

Emily padded down the steps in her stocking feet and caught sight of Birdie sitting cross-legged on the sofa. Her aunt had changed into jeans and an old paisley shirt that was frayed with all the washings, but she loved the memories associated with the shirt so wouldn't part with it. She'd angled her body toward Archer, who'd taken off his crisp button-down shirt and wore a white T-shirt. Both sat with their backs to her, giving her a chance to study them for a moment.

"I feel so guilty, and I hate the toll it's taking on Emily," Birdie said softly.

Emily was pleased to see Birdie was coherent again, but her dear aunt had nothing to feel sorry for. Emily was a different story. She'd gone off on Archer when he'd simply done a sweet thing, and he didn't deserve her wrath. He was nothing like the men her mother brought home.

And that was the problem. He made her think she could successfully have a fulfilling relationship with a man. A man like Archer?

"Emily has so much to deal with taking up my slack," Birdie continued. "If only I could do more."

Archer gently took Birdie's hand in his. "You can't think that way. You didn't ask for this."

At the incredible softness and compassion in Archer's tone, Emily yearned to see the expression on his face.

"She has an unfathomable love for you," he

continued. "That's clear for anyone to see and she'll do whatever she needs to make sure you're okay."

"She thinks she owes me from the past, but she doesn't. I'm the one in debt to her."

He released Birdie's hands and sat back. "How's that?"

"When she was thirteen her mother's current boyfriend didn't want a teenager around, so her mother shipped her off to me. Emily thought she was imposing, but truth is, I was lonely on my own. I'd never married. Just didn't find the right guy. So I had no children of my own. But I longed for family and prayed for God to fulfill my wishes."

Birdie shook her head, her silvery curls bouncing. "Then along came Emily. Stubborn and so tough on the surface. She had to be to survive her parents' constant arguments before her dad walked out. Then the parade of men her mother took up with. But under it all was—is—the sweetest, most compassionate person I know. I've told her so many times how blessed I am to have her in my life, but I'm not sure she ever believed me."

Emily's heart constricted with love, and she dropped to the stairs. She had no idea Birdie felt this way. Sure, Emily knew her aunt loved her unconditionally and had always said that she was thankful to have Emily in her life, but Emily honestly thought Birdie was just saying that to make her feel good.

And not finding the right guy? Birdie had never mentioned that either. Emily thought it was a lifestyle choice Birdie had made. Emily also had no clue her aunt had been so lonely.

Knowing this was a game changer. If Emily *had* known, she might not have patterned her own life after Birdie's. Vowing never to get involved. To be self-sufficient and live on her own.

One thing Emily did know. She couldn't let another minute go by without telling Birdie how much she appreciated her.

She stepped into the room, sat on the coffee table and clasped Birdie's hands in hers. "I overheard you. I believe you really wanted me here, but I'm still the most blessed. You gave me so much more than a roof over my head, Aunt Birdie. You gave me a home and taught me about love."

Birdie squeezed Emily's hands. "But now—with this mess—you have surely gotten the bad end of the stick."

"I'll take any end of the stick if it means you're in my life."

A faraway look claimed Birdie's face. "God really turned a bad situation in your life into something wonderful for both of us, didn't He?"

"He did."

"It's a good reminder. I need to stop worrying about how you'll fare with my disease. He always turns everything to good."

"But how?" Emily freed her hands and sat back. "How can He possibly turn your Alzheimer's to good?"

"Emily," Birdie scolded. "Where's the faith I taught you to live by?"

"I'm sorry, but I just don't see any positive from this except that because I came to live here, I'm able to spend more time with you."

"That's a blessing to me, and you are making my life so much better. Even if I don't remember it much of the time, I'm grateful." She scooted to the edge of the sofa and kissed Emily on the forehead. "I'm really tired. If you don't mind, I'm going to go back to bed."

"Sure," Emily said and made sure not to sound disappointed. She had so little quality time left with her aunt that she hated to waste any of it to sleep, but Birdie knew what her body needed.

Emily drew her aunt into her arms and hugged her like she might never see her again. And who knew—with the Alzheimer's Emily very well might never see this Birdie again.

"I love you, Birdie," she whispered.

"And I love you, sweetheart." She pulled

back, stroked the side of Emily's face for a moment before heading up the stairs.

Tears stung Emily's eyes. The room swimming in front of her. She wasn't sure what to say or do. If Archer wasn't sitting on the sofa, she might let the tears take her and have a big old cry.

"These moments of clarity are a blessing, too," he said quietly.

"But not for long," Emily muttered more to herself than to him as she thought about how these moments were fleeting. "Especially with the disease progressing and we're about to be thrown out on our ear."

She blinked hard to stem the tears. She had to do something or she'd lose it in front of Archer, and she feared once the dam burst, she'd never be able to stop it. Especially if he held her. Then she wouldn't want to come up for air at all.

She took a deep breath and willed away the tears as she tried to think of a good reason to leave the room. *The garden.* She forgot to water the garden. The one place she could be alone to think. The one place she found contentment and peace because God seemed closer there. The place where, if He decided to end this silence, she would find a way out of this mess.

"It's getting late," she said and started for the doorway, then remembered she'd wanted to apologize to Archer. No. Not now. Not when she would fall apart. He deserved her attention, not her tears. She'd speak to him first thing in the morning.

She took one last look at him, but a lone tear escaped and rolled down her cheek before she could look away.

"Emily," he said and quickly approached her.

At his tender expression, she remained riveted in place. He continued gazing into her eyes as he wiped away a second tear.

"Emily," he said again, this time his voice was choked with emotion.

Powerless to look away, she stared up at him, her heart longing for more from this man— longing to bring these unspoken feelings between them to light. But she couldn't give in.

"I have to go," she mumbled, then rushed away.

She hurried through the foyer and dining room to the kitchen, where she slipped into her gardening clogs and grabbed a flashlight. Hopefully he'd think she was taking the back stairway. She listened to see if he followed her, as he'd been her shadow for two days now, but she didn't hear a thing so she stepped outside and down the path.

She found silence. Blessed silence save the

frogs' rumbling croaks and an owl hooting in the distance. Her tears ran over her cheeks, but she kept going, swinging the flashlight down the path lined with trellises holding clematis and honeysuckle vines. She'd added the trellises and vines to camouflage the ugly chicken wire fence she'd erected to keep critters out of the vegetables.

She inhaled a deep whiff of the pungent fragrance that blessed her every time she stepped into her garden. She tried to put everything but her garden out of her mind as she clicked on the lights she'd strung along the garden perimeter.

Time spent in God's glorious creation often had such a calming effect on her, but tonight she kept thinking about Birdie saying she really would have married if the right man had come along.

Is a relationship worth the risk of ending up like my mother?

At the stream running through the property, she slipped off her shoes and dipped a bucket into the cool water bubbling down the hill. She stood there, the water gently swirling over large boulders and around her feet. All her troubles swirled out of her brain, and it was as if her entire body was sighing with joy.

Emily scooped the bucket full, then turned

back to the tomato plants, ten in all to feed their guests should business pick up. She bent low to the rich soil she'd worked with compost to produce a luscious organic crop. Normally she used a hose, but tonight in addition to the mental healing properties of the moving water, she wanted to keep the water off the leaves to prevent diseases. She went back to the stream, enjoying the cool water on her feet. She stooped with her bucket.

The grass swished behind her. Fearing an animal, she rose up.

Hard hands landed on her shoulders and gave a solid shove.

Her feet slipped. The bucket flew. She lost her balance and fell forward. She tried to stop her fall, but slippery fingers gave way on the mossy boulders, and she smacked her head against the slimy stone.

She thought she cried out, but she wasn't sure.

All she knew was pain. Curiosity and confusion.

And fear. For herself, but mostly for Birdie. If this was a fatal blow, Emily would leave Birdie alone in a world of confusion.

But then… Emily knew nothing as the world went black and the same cool water that had refreshed her moments ago rose up to cocoon around her.

* * *

Emily's cry split the air and then a splash sounded through the silent night.

Archer didn't know if he should believe his ears or not.

She'd left the house without his knowledge, but he saw her crossing the lawn. He suspected she needed time alone in her garden sanctuary. That didn't mean he'd let her go wandering around at night alone when a stalker was still out there, most likely watching her every move. So he followed and hung near the garden entrance.

There. Another sound. Footsteps running through the woods that abutted her garden.

Baumann? No, the steps were sure and strong, not halting and broken. Was it Emily running from danger? Or Fallon or even Taylor running from her?

Archer shot around the honeysuckle vines, adrenaline stealing his breath.

"Emily!" he called out, but quickly spotted her lying in the stream, water swirling over her.

"No!" Fear threatened to swamp him. He plunged into the frigid water.

Please, Father, please. Let her be okay.

He wanted to jerk her into his arms, but his training taught him to assess her injuries before moving her. He squatted next to her. Checked her airway. Her head was turned to the side and she was breathing.

Thank You, Father.

But she was also unconscious. He checked for other external injuries. A quick sweep of his hand over her head and sticky blood coated his palm.

Had the person he'd heard fleeing cracked her over the head, or had she fallen into the water and connected with a boulder?

Fallon. It had to be Fallon. Or Taylor.

He didn't know.

"Emily," he said in a whisper.

No response.

"Emily, wake up." He put authority into his voice.

No movement.

What should he do?

Call 911, his training suggested, but it would take forever to get an ambulance out there.

He didn't think about it any longer. With precious moments ticking away, he gently lifted her into his arms, making sure to support her head, and trudged through the water, being sure his feet found solid ground.

He climbed up the bank to the garden. Pummeled up the path. Put Emily in the backseat of his car and opened the driver's door, but came to a stop. He couldn't leave Birdie alone. He bolted for the house.

Inside he stood where he could still keep an eye on Emily and yelled up the stairs, "Birdie, get up. Emily's been hurt, and we have to take her to the hospital."

He heard her stirring. It would take her a few moments to get ready so he jerked out his phone and made a call to 911 to let them know he was a deputy and to prepare for Emily's arrival at the ER.

Birdie stepped into the hallway and he nearly fell to the floor in praise when he saw that she was dressed and cognizant. "Where's Emily?"

"In the car," he said. "We have to go."

He didn't wait for her to follow, but charged out. At the car, he opened the back door for Birdie. His gaze landed on Emily. Limp. Looking lifeless. What would he do if he lost her?

"Oh, my sweetheart," Birdie cried out as she climbed into the backseat to cradle Emily's head on her lap.

Archer prayed again, started the car and floored it, peeling down the driveway and spraying rocks.

"Calm down," Birdie commanded in a tone he hadn't heard from her before. "It won't do any good if you crash."

Archer took her warning to heart and instead of careening around the corner to the main road as he'd do on an urgent code in his patrol car, he took the turn carefully.

"Tell me what happened," Birdie said.

"I'm not sure. I was at the entrance of the garden when I heard a splash of water and found Emily had hit her head on a boulder in the river."

"Did she fall or was she…" Her voice dropped off.

"Pushed? I don't know."

Birdie fell silent, and Archer glanced at her in the mirror. She was gazing at Emily, her expression tender. She loved Emily unconditionally. Lived to see Emily happy and thriving.

Then it hit him, the realization, like a punch to the gut.

Darcie was right. This was what he wanted, what he was searching for. He'd longed for such caring in his life, when he'd had only minimal attention from his parents and paid servants, and that often didn't last long. Sure he had his fellow teammates now, but friendship went only so far. He wanted more, but finding it and losing it was almost as scary as not having it at all.

He glanced in the rearview mirror. Saw Emily cradled in Birdie's arms. He may have saved her from drowning, but she still wasn't out of the woods, and if he didn't get her to the hospital soon, he could lose her.

Father, please, Archer begged. *Let us arrive in time to save her life.*

THIRTEEN

Pain pulled Emily from the dark and up a tunnel toward bustling sounds and a strong antiseptic smell. Her head throbbed and she didn't want to open her eyes under the ER's bright lights, but she forced them open. The doctor had told her that she had a concussion, and because she'd lost consciousness, he wanted to keep her overnight for observation. There was no way she would stay in the hospital when Birdie had once again retreated into her world and was already sleeping in a strange bed.

When Emily came to in the car, Birdie had been communicative, but as they neared the ER, her mind drifted off, and by the time they arrived, Birdie was firmly lodged in the past again. Emily thought it better if Birdie didn't come back to the examination rooms in her state, so Archer offered to sit with her. Another thing for which Emily was now in Archer's debt.

A knock thumped on the door, the sound

grinding into her skull and sending a stabbing pain through her head.

She fought back the pain and plastered a smile on her face. "Come in."

The door opened and Archer stood looking at her, his gaze roving over her. He crossed his arms over his broad chest and leaned against the doorjamb for a moment, his gaze fixing on her eyes. She was so happy to see him and she didn't want to look away. She wanted him to cross the room and hold her. To promise her fall into the water was a bad dream.

"You're awake. Had us real worried for a while there, you know." He suddenly pulled his gaze free and stepped over to her bedside. "Before you ask about Birdie, I just had to see how you're doing, and a nurse is sitting with her."

She nodded her understanding, but pain stopped her midnod. "I'm about as good as a klutz can be after falling into a stream and clunking her head."

"So you fell?"

"Yes, of course," she replied but then thought about the accident. "Honestly, I don't remember what happened, but what else could it be?" A bout of nausea threatened and she closed her eyes to ward it off.

"I think you had help."

She flashed her eyes open. "What?"

"I followed you down to the stream. I didn't actually see you fall, but I heard the splash. I also heard someone running away in the woods."

"Who?"

"The footsteps weren't halting like I'd expect to hear from Baumann so I'm liking Fannon for this."

"Stan?" She raised her eyebrows and even that little movement sent pain radiating through her skull, making her wince.

"You're in pain. Let me get the doctor for you."

"I'm fine." She waved off his concern even as her heart warmed at his attention. "You're sure about Stan?"

"As sure as I can be without any actual evidence to prove his guilt."

"But what about Lance?"

"I don't like the guy, but I just can't see him getting his hands dirty."

"But you did suggest he could have hired someone, right?"

He nodded. "Any reason you're hoping Taylor's behind this?"

"Stan lost his fiancée, and I hate that he might be lashing out in pain and would end up in jail for it. Taylor, on the other hand, is someone who I could see doing something unethical and ending up in jail."

Archer worked the muscles in his jaw. "Either way, we need to find who was on your property this late at night."

"How?"

"I've already called Jake. He's arranged to have Carothers and a forensic team dispatched to your property. Maybe they'll turn up something we can use and narrow down the suspect list."

"But what if it I really did slip?"

"Then there won't be any evidence to process. But if you didn't…" He sat on the edge of her bed, the shifting of the mattress making the world spin.

He leaned close and brushed his thumb over her cheek, then cupped the side of her face, sending her world spinning for a far different reason. She forgot about the hospital. Forgot about her pain. Forgot about a man trying to kill her.

She closed her eyes and leaned into his hand to relish the warmth of his touch. The simple act of caring put a crack in years of certainty that she didn't need or want a man in her life.

This was what she'd been missing. What she'd vowed never to have. What she thought Birdie didn't want. But now…now she knew Birdie had sought it out, too.

Emily wanted to succumb to her emotions,

open her eyes and kiss Archer, but an old ache manifested itself in her gut. Letting go was exactly the kind of thing that her mother fell victim to over and over and over again. Emily may now understand that having a man in her life could be a good thing, but that didn't mean she'd make a hasty decision and throw herself at the first man who captured her interest.

She opened her eyes and moved back, the effort painful, but allowing Archer to continue to touch her could end up being far more painful. She met his gaze. "You were saying something about the accident."

He continued to focus on her for a long moment, and she felt like squirming, but stayed strong.

He took a breath. Let it out. "If you didn't fall, then our suspect has come out in the open and made a blatant attempt on your life."

All the warm, fuzzy feelings she was still fighting evaporated. "Then we need to get back to the B and B as soon as possible and help the forensic team search."

His shoulders went up into a rigid line. "We'll go when the doctor discharges you and not a moment before."

She gathered as much determination as she could manage and fired it in a look back at him.

"Fine," he grumbled. "I'm overstepping my

bounds, but when I found you in the water…"
He shook his head, his fingers curling into rock-
hard fists. "If the guy who pushed you was
standing there, I could have killed him with my
bare hands."

His vehement response shocked her. Maybe
he wasn't the man she thought he was. "Do you
usually get this angry on the job?"

His nostrils flared, and he locked gazes with
her. "I think we both know this is more than a
job for me."

"It is but—"

"I have your discharge orders." A nurse bus-
tled into the room, interrupting their discussion.

Emily was glad for the reprieve, and yet, she
wanted to hear what Archer was about to say,
but she also knew it was better to let this lie and
not enter into a personal discussion.

The tall nurse, wearing a baby blue set of
scrubs, set down a tablet on the table and looked
at Archer. "I'm glad you're here."

"Okay," he said, looking confused.

The nurse flipped through Emily's chart.
"You are Archer Reed, right?"

He nodded.

"And you're the one designated to keep an eye
on Emily tonight?"

He glanced at Emily, curiosity burning in
his eyes.

Heat crept up her face. "The doctor said I needed someone at the house with me or he wouldn't let me leave. Birdie can't do it so I..."

"I see," Archer responded, but didn't expound so she had no idea what he was thinking.

"That settled?" the nurse asked.

"There was never a question," he said firmly. "I'll be there. You can count on it."

Emily liked the certainty in his voice. Liked that he was committed to helping her. Something to add to her list to guard against before she craved his company on a regular basis. It was likely her feelings and the desire to have him around stemmed more from taking on the immense task of caring for Birdie alone more than anything. She shouldn't confuse it for something else and do something foolish like fall for him.

The nurse launched into signs and warning symptoms to watch for and gave directions on when and where to call the doctor if needed. Emily listened carefully, but Archer seemed to memorize everything she said, even asking for clarification on a few items before the nurse departed, leaving them alone.

Emily waited for Archer to continue their discussion, but he didn't speak. Good. Emily would have shut him down anyway. She wasn't about to return to their prior conversation and put herself in a position where she had to be careful about every word.

She closed her eyes, waited for the hospital to finish her discharge papers and soon found herself back at the B and B, where she settled Birdie into the guest room. Emily sat in the chair until her aunt was snoring softly, then crept out of the bedroom. Emily would return to sit with Birdie for the rest of the night, but Archer had joined Jake and the detective at the stream, and she wanted to know what they'd found.

She stepped outside and let the cool breeze play over her body. The moon had broken through the clouds and shone bright, illuminating the property. Normally, she enjoyed the idyllic view looking over the valley with tall pines framing the picture, but tonight, a crime scene van plus the detective's and Jake's car spoiled the setting.

She caught sight of her guests standing on the small porch, peering into the distance. She had to do some damage control.

Still dizzy, she grabbed the handrail and slowly took the steps. She focused on the guests to forget the pain brought on by moving. An older couple, Patsy and Wallace Becker from Minnesota were friendly and gracious. She was tall and gangly. He was short and wide, looking like a heavy anvil had fallen on his head and compressed his body. The pair might be opposites in appearance, but their lifelong love for each other shone in their actions.

"I'm sorry about the chaos," Emily said as she joined them.

"We heard that you got hurt." Patsy let her gaze roam over Emily from head to toe.

"It's nothing."

Wallace puffed up his chest. "If we're in danger here, we need to know."

"There's no danger." *To anyone but me.* "So please, if you can, ignore the vehicles and go back to bed."

"We do need our sleep," Patsy said. "We're planning on hiking the gorge tomorrow."

Emily was glad to have guests, but after the latest incident, she was happy to hear they'd be away for most of the day tomorrow. "Why don't I make a picnic basket for your hike? That way you can have lunch and enjoy the view."

Patsy smiled. "That would be nice."

"Good. I'll see you at breakfast, then," Emily said, backing away and signaling the end of their conversation.

She crossed the lot and could feel the Beckers watching her, but she didn't turn and acknowledge them. Instead, she took the trail to her garden and inhaled the sweet honeysuckle for comfort. The sounds of bubbling water filtered up the incline, bringing back her fall.

Why couldn't she remember it? Had she been pushed and she was blocking it out to keep from remembering the terror?

She rounded the corner and found Archer and Jake standing on the riverbank staring down at a man in white coveralls. He was lifting something white from the soil. As she drew closer, she thought it looked like plaster. She'd seen enough TV crime shows to know they'd taken a mold of something.

"What's that?" she asked as she approached.

Archer turned to look at her. "You should be resting."

"Don't worry so much. I'm fine." She smiled to emphasize her words. "So what are you looking at?"

"A man's shoe print."

The tech stood up. "Hiker. Size eleven I'd say. Not something you'd wear if you thought you might need to take a jog through the woods."

"You'll run it through OSP's database, right?" Jake asked.

Archer faced Emily. "The Oregon State Police keep an extensive database of shoes and tires, giving us a good chance at determining the manufacturer and style that fits this print."

The tech pointed at the cast. "If we can find

the shoe, matching it to the unique features of the cast should be easy."

"I don't understand," Emily said, wondering if this was a simple concept that she couldn't grasp because of the injury or if it was more complicated.

"The cast shows the sole's inside edge is worn down so the guy overpronates. Means his foot turns in more than normal when he walks or runs, putting excess wear on the inside of the shoe."

"So what you all are saying is that you think there was a man here tonight," Emily clarified. "Couldn't it be an old print?"

"Ignoring the fact that I suspect not many men stand at the river in your private garden sanctuary," Archer said, "if the print was old it would have filled with water and been degraded. This is fresh and prime."

He was right. Men didn't come down there. At least not that she knew of.

A sharp pain stabbed through her head, and she closed her eyes. She listened to the gentle lapping of the stream against the bank. The whisper of the wind through the trees. Smelled the sweet scent of honeysuckle traveling on the breeze.

Her mind suddenly flashed in brilliant colors, like a flickering video. Flashes of the water. The feeling of hands on her shoulders. Falling. The rock in front. Trying to turn to avoid it. Her face in the water and thoughts that it was the end, and her beloved Birdie would be all alone to cope with her dreaded disease as Emily blanked out.

"He pushed me." She forced the words from her throat. "I remember now. His hands on my shoulders." Despite the muggy heat, she shivered. "The hands were big. Thick. So I know it was a guy."

"Apparently a guy who wears size-eleven hikers," Archer said, barely controlled anger in his tone. "Shoes I will find, and this man will pay."

So much anger today. She was worried about him. Wanted to take his hand. To help calm him down. But they were with his law enforcement coworkers, and she doubted he'd want her to coddle him in front of them.

Besides, thoughts like that only led to caring about someone and only a few hours ago she'd reaffirmed her stance that she wasn't going there.

Not tonight. Not ever.

FOURTEEN

Emily tried to put the previous night's incident out of her mind as she packed the picnic basket for the Beckers in the B and B kitchen. Normally she loved working in the big kitchen, but her head ached from last night. Fortunately, the dizziness was gone, but the side of her head remained swollen and tender. And if that didn't distract her enough, Archer paced like a caged animal in the kitchen, making her nervous. She'd asked him to sit down, and he did. For a moment. Then he hopped to his feet and started pacing again.

She loaded fresh fruit, homemade potato salad and thick turkey sandwiches on whole grain bread. All she had to add were dishes and a tablecloth and she'd be ready to hand over the basket to the Beckers.

Archer marched past her.

Her irritation mounted. "Your pacing is driving me nuts."

"Sorry. I guess I'm kind of jittery. I want to find the creep terrorizing you, but we don't have anything other than the boot print to go on."

"How long will it take to process the print?"

"Jake texted me an hour ago to say the lab guys were running it through the database, so I should hear something any second. Guess that's why I'm so jumpy."

His phone signaled a text, and he shoved his hand into his pocket to draw it out.

She watched him as he read it and his eyes lit up.

"It's a picture of the boot." He crossed the room to her. "Does this look like the one Fallon was wearing when we talked to him?"

He held out his phone and for a moment, she didn't want to look, but she forced her focus to the screen.

She stared at the picture, but didn't know what to make of it. "Yes, he was wearing them, but half the guys in Oregon Free have a pair of these."

"Say what?" Archer's voice rose.

"One of our members is a designer at Nike. He arranged for our members to get a good deal on this boot."

"How many guys have them?"

"From what I can remember from a hike we

all took a while back, most of the guys were wearing them."

"Okay so we have a lot of guys who own this boot," Archer said, sounding like he was thinking aloud. "Not a problem. Remember last night when the tech mentioned overpronating?" Renewed excitement was building in his voice. "We all walk differently and wear down our soles at a different rate, so our shoe prints are about as unique as a fingerprint."

"Which means even if a lot of the guys have these boots, an ID can still be made," she said, catching his drift.

"Plus you remember them taking soil samples last night?"

She nodded.

"Most of the soil around here is what you would expect to find in this area of the county. So if our suspect picked it up on his boots when he pushed you, even if we located his boots and they had soil particulates from your garden in the treads, it wouldn't tie him to this specific location. But if he carried soil on his boots from another location to the stream, it might be mixed with the soil we gathered. If so, we could match the unique blend to soil found in the suspect's boot treads and that could be another way to identify him."

"So we should have a suspect soon, then."

He frowned. "Problem is, we'll either need our suspects to willingly hand over their boots or probable cause to confiscate the boots for comparison. Right now, all we have are suspicions and little else."

Archer's phone chimed in his hand and he looked at the screen. "It's from Jake again. He just got an update on the last victim from the mall shooting. He's out of the ICU, and the doctors are optimistic for a full recovery."

"Praise God for that," she exclaimed and took a moment to silently thank the good Lord for His answers to their prayers before turning back to the basket.

"On the negative side, this means Withrow will be released from jail sooner," Archer added. "But he'll be brought up on attempted murder and a plethora of other charges. He'll most certainly be going to prison for a long time and can no longer hurt you."

She was glad to hear that, but… "After hearing what the group said about Stan last night, I wouldn't be surprised if Delmar connects with Stan and manages to convince him to do his dirty work for him."

Archer grimaced. "That's still a possibility. One we don't need to think about unless we're told that Stan visits Withrow or calls him."

She tried to put the thought out of her mind as

she placed napkins on top of the old-fashioned wicker basket and latched the lid. "There. It's ready."

Archer tapped a finger on a container of potato salad she'd made first thing that morning. "Please tell me we're going to be eating this same meal for our lunch."

"So you like potato salad?"

"Growing up, we had fancy meals. Nothing as American as potato salad, and I've come to appreciate some of the more basic recipes." He grinned, erasing the tension in the room. He nodded at the other container. "I like those brownies more."

He tried to open the container and she swatted his hand. He snatched it back, and his grin widened.

The moment was so intimate, like a couple at home, relaxed and having fun with each other, that she grabbed containers and rushed to the refrigerator before she let herself want that very thing.

She stowed the containers and took a moment to clear her thoughts before going back to the island. "I need to deliver the basket to the Beckers. I suppose you're planning to walk with me."

"Did you even need to ask?"

She rolled her eyes and grabbed the basket handle, but he took it, his hand brushing against hers. She was so aware of his touch and her need to avoid it, that she nearly bolted out the door and down the steps.

The wind had picked up and whisked over them as they crossed the lawn. The sun was warm and yet not stifling this early in the day. Birds chirped from the trees, and if this man who was getting under her skin despite her defenses wasn't walking beside her, she'd take a moment to enjoy the weather.

"It's a beautiful day," she said, hoping the small talk would redirect her thoughts.

"For a day out in the country, sure."

She looked up at him. "Not that all Oregonians like the outdoors, but I'm suspecting you're not from our fair state."

"New York City born and raised."

"Wow." Her feet came to a halt, and she gaped at him for a moment. "Talk about the direct opposite of Oregon. How did you end up out here?"

He stared at her with a funny look in his eyes that she couldn't decipher. "As I mentioned, I wanted to find a job where I could make a difference."

"They have no police in the Big Apple?" she joked.

A curtain came down over his eyes, dulling the electric-blue color. He planted his feet. His jaw squared obstinately, he gestured ahead. "We should get out of the open."

Fine. He didn't want to talk about his past. She got it, but she didn't like it. Not one bit. Most of the men her mom dated were the same. They seemed to be a perfect choice at first, and then, once she'd invited them into their home, the secrets came out. The abuser. The drinker. The gambler. All of them had something that her mother chose to overlook and keep overlooking until they decided to leave.

Emily could never trust a man who wasn't open.

She stepped off and he kept up with her as she hurried across the yard.

A scream originating from the cottage suddenly pierced the silence.

"Where's Birdie?" Archer asked, already picking up speed.

"Sleeping at the main house," Emily answered.

"Then it has to be your guests."

"No…" Emily whispered, but knew he was right.

It was bad enough that someone was targeting her, but her guests didn't deserve to get caught in the crossfire. Guilt snapped at her as she ran with Archer to the door, her head throbbing with every step. He pounded hard.

Wallace soon answered and made eye contact with Emily. "Good. You're here." He stood back and let them in.

They found Patsy cringing behind the sofa, her mouth hanging open. She looked up, terror rampant in her gaze. "He was there. Outside that window. Wearing a black mask and then he stepped inside. He had a gun. A real gun. He pointed it at me. Then backed out and took off."

Emily fired a horrified look at Archer and implored him to help.

"I'll check it out. You all need to move away from any windows. The bathroom is perfect." He drew his sidearm and looked at them pointedly until they tromped to the bathroom.

Inside the small room, Wallace spun on her. "What's going on here?"

Emily opened her mouth to reply to his demand for answers, but suddenly everything that had occurred in the past few days hit her hard and she couldn't form any words. Could only offer a silent plea.

Help me, Father. Please. I don't know what to do. I'm at the end of my rope.

Archer stood next to Emily at the cottage door as the Beckers stormed toward their car. He'd made a thorough search of the property, but struck out in finding the masked man and had called in reinforcements. The uniforms had also searched the property to no avail and Carothers had taken statements while forensics searched for evidence. Patsy gave a description of the man's size, which fit Fannon's build, but it fit Lance Taylor, as well. The only suspect ruled out at this point was Baumann because the man didn't limp.

At her car, Patsy turned and fired an angry look at Emily. Emily looked like she might crumple on the spot so Archer moved closer, hoping his nearness would give her strength to weather yet another storm.

"Our stay may have been free," Pasty said through clenched teeth, "but expect to hear from our attorney. Taking guests while you were in danger is reckless. Very reckless. You will pay for our emotional distress."

A small gasp came from Emily, but she recovered quickly and apologized again. Archer had come to know her well enough to tell that she was more upset that her guests had suffered because of her than the threat of a lawsuit.

The engine revved on their modest sedan and Wallace peeled out faster than necessary.

Emily rubbed her forehead, her fingers roving toward the bruised side. She winced, then dropped her hand and looked so defeated. He wanted to help her get through another incident, but he could think of only two options open to him. The first was to hold her until this mess was resolved. The second, to find the guy who was making her life a living nightmare.

He couldn't do the first without telling her about his background. About his money. Having gotten to know her, he was sure under normal circumstances his money would mean nothing. But her life was far from normal now. After the loss of additional guests, she was even more desperate, and desperation made people do outlandish things. So he'd keep his mouth shut and work on option two. Find the guy.

She took a deep breath and let it out. "I really don't think I can take any more."

"You're strong, honey," he soothed. "And you'll get through this for Birdie's sake. I know you will."

She seemed taken aback by him calling her honey, but it had just slipped out and he wouldn't apologize. She chewed on her lip. "Maybe this is God's way of telling me that Birdie and I need to throw in the towel and close the B and B."

"But you still don't want to give up," he said.

"No." She faced the building and tears pooled in her eyes. "This is my home. The only home I've known. I can't imagine it not being part of my life."

A physical ache clutched Archer's heart. He'd

warned himself to stay away. To keep from getting involved, but he couldn't stand by any longer and let her suffer all alone. He reached out for her, laying his hands on her upper arms and drawing her closer. He expected her to resist, but she willingly let him pull her into his warm embrace, and rested her head against him.

He tightened his arms around her and she snuggled even closer, burrowing her head on his chest. It felt so right, natural, to hold her, and he hoped she felt the same way. Though he doubted she was thinking about how they fit together. Not now when her shoulders shook and the tears started flowing.

He reached into his pocket and drew out a handkerchief. He handed it to her.

A surprised look flashed across her face.

"My upbringing again," he said drolly. "I was taught never to leave home without one."

She wiped her eyes, then stared up at him with a wobbly smile. "You're this strong, tough guy and then you go and do something like carry a handkerchief. I love all the nuances to your personality."

His heart soared at her words, but he didn't know what to say in return without moving them closer to a relationship that neither of them wanted or needed.

Her smile vanished and she looked down,

then tapped a large wet ring on his chest. "I'm sorry I made a mess of your shirt. I know how much you like to be neat and pressed."

"You've picked up on that, huh?" He grinned.

"Would be hard not to." She laughed, but then their eyes met in a lingering gaze. He searched deep within hers and she didn't back away. The laughter stilled between them. Fire burned across the space. His heart rate skyrocketed, and he tightened his hold before lowering his head, thinking of nothing but what it was going to feel like to kiss her.

His lips met hers, the spark between them everything he'd imagined and more. She didn't resist, and for a moment, she even deepened the kiss, giving him hope that she felt the same way he did. That she wanted the kiss to go on forever.

She suddenly pulled back. He whipped his eyes open to look at her.

Unease had darkened her eyes, and she planted her hands on his chest, then pushed out of his arms. "I should check on Birdie."

She walked away, moving toward the main house.

"Emily, wait," he called after her.

She didn't stop, and in fact, it looked like she was picking up her pace.

His emotions firing on high, he charged after her and gently turned her by the shoulder to face him. He knew the next words from his mouth were important, and yet, his mind went blank and he simply stared at her.

She jerked her gaze away. "I really have to get going."

"I can lend you the money you need to keep the business going," he blurted out and regretted the words the instant they came out.

"Money?" She lurched back. "I can't take your money."

"Sure you can," he rushed on, hoping to keep her there so he could explain. "My family is quite wealthy. I have a huge trust fund just sitting around. I don't need it and you could use it. You can pay me back or not. It's up to you."

"No," she said, her eyes filled with confusion. She continued to peer up at him and her eyes darkened into a similar gut-wrenching pain he'd seen when Withrow first attacked.

He'd hurt her. Of course, he had. He should have told her about his money right up front. He'd kept a big part of himself from her when she'd been forthcoming about her past.

"I've got to go." She marched toward the house.

He trailed behind, keeping his head on a swivel, watching for danger.

He'd really botched that. Meant an end to anything between them in more ways than one. Exactly what he'd first claimed he'd wanted, but now the thought simply twisted his gut into a hard knot.

FIFTEEN

Emily checked on Birdie, who'd thankfully slept through another incident. Hoping to avoid Archer, Emily took the back stairs down to the office. She was hyped up and she couldn't sit still so she paced the room. Back and forth. Thoughts firing through her mind as quickly as her feet moved across the floor.

"Trust fund, right," she mumbled.

She was such a fool. After Darcie's earlier comment, Emily thought he might be in financial trouble, too, and then it turns out he's swimming in money? Money he could have already offered. Not that she'd ever consider taking it, but he'd kept it to himself as if he needed to hide it.

A secret. Like the men in her mother's life.

"Ha!" Just the opposite of her mother's financial issues, but he hadn't shared this important part of his life. She'd given him plenty of opportunities to mention his past, to mention the money, but he sidestepped everything.

What else might he be hiding?

She stopped at the window and gazed over the lawn. Her eyes taking in the property she loved so dearly. The property that even her best efforts hadn't been able to save.

The lack of money was a problem. A big one. But it wasn't the only thing weighing heavy on her mind. Admitting to herself that she couldn't save the place. Couldn't control the B and B or Birdie's illness. Couldn't gain control of her life any longer. Or even manage her feelings for Archer. That was an even bigger issue.

She'd tried so hard. Planned. Scheduled. Organized. Found the best doctors for Birdie. She'd done her best. Tried her hardest. But her best wasn't good enough.

Why, Lord? Why?

A shadow darkened the doorway and Archer stood waiting. "Can I come in?"

She nodded and forced herself not to resume pacing to keep him from seeing how unsettled she was.

He moved close enough for her to catch a hint of the soap he favored, and he appraised her with perceptive eyes digging deep. "You doing okay?"

She wanted to toss out a smart-aleck response

so he would leave and she wouldn't be tempted to snake her arms around his neck and finish the kiss she'd run from. But he didn't deserve a flip answer when he was genuinely interested in her well-being.

She took a breath. Blew it out. "I'm doing better and I'll go on fighting for Birdie. I want so badly to succeed for her. I think trying to save her home is the least I can do for all she's given me. I've tried so hard, but..."

"But problems have hit you at every turn." He reached for her hand.

She wasn't at all opposed to his touch, but for precisely that reason she stepped back.

Her actions earned her a raise of his eyebrow as his hand fell to his side. "You can let go of that iron control, you know. Maybe let someone else help you for once."

"Easy to say, but hard to do when it's ingrained behavior," she said honestly.

"Tell me about it." His words were more of a command than anything.

She thought about not responding, but she didn't like the way he'd kept his past a secret and she wouldn't do the same thing to him.

"I told you about my parents," she started. "About my mom and her many men. Controlling my environment was the only way to coexist with the latest guy. Dictating my own moves and other people to the extent that I could. My circumstances."

"And you never relaxed even when you came to live with Birdie?"

"A bit, I guess, but when bad things happen, my go-to move is still to take over."

"You mean like right now?" he asked softly.

"Exactly. If I could just get a handle on these things, I—"

"Could what? Fix it? That's all you've been trying to do since I met you, and it's not working so well. Maybe it's time to change tactics."

She clenched her hands and released. "I just need to try harder. Tighten the reins more."

"Or not," he said, sounding so sure of himself. "You can't control others and what they do. I know. I lived it firsthand with my family." Pain lit in his eyes for a moment before he cleared it. He rested on the corner of the desk and seemed to be at war with how or even if he should continue.

The air was tinged with tension. She was tempted to jump in, ask about his family, but after hiding his money from her, he willingly had to open up about his past, too. Otherwise, how could she trust him?

He looked down at his hands resting on his knees. "My dad wanted me to work for his stock brokerage firm. I didn't want to spend my life in finance, but I caved to his demands and got the MBA he wanted. After a few months of working for him, I knew I couldn't do it. I had to follow my own path so I quit the firm."

His foot started swinging and his long fingers clasped his leg like a vise. "We argued that day and for the next two years. He couldn't fathom telling his friends and associates that his son was a deputy. It was more about how people perceived him than if I was happy."

He shook his head in slow, sorrowful arcs. "When Dad realized that I was never coming back, he and my mom turned their backs on me. I reach out to them off and on, but I get the same cold shoulder and we still don't talk." He finally looked up and met her gaze head-on. "It took some time, but I finally figured out that I'd done nothing wrong. It was all on my parents and I couldn't change their minds. It was in God's hands alone."

She'd been so wrapped up in her own mess of a life, and he'd seemed like he was on an even keel, that she never even considered that he might be going through something like this.

"I'm so sorry, Archer." She rested a hand on his arm. "Guess we both know what it's like to have parents let us down."

"Learn from my situation, Emily," he implored. "Trust God and know that whatever happens it will all be okay." He pressed a hand over hers.

She felt the warmth of his hands, the urgency in his words, but… "It sounds so simple."

"Simple? No. We're always going to have trouble and want to fight it ourselves. We're wired that way, but if we let God take control and trust Him, He promises peace in the midst of the pain."

"I know the verse you're talking about, and trust me—" she shook her head "—I want peace in my life. How I want it."

"But?" he asked, his gaze riveted on her.

Her heart ached and she wanted to surrender her concerns to God. But the potential loss of Birdie, of the B and B, was too painful for her to fathom leaving it up to Him alone. "But I'm not as strong as you are. I can't let go. Not now."

Maybe never.

Archer was a hypocrite. He knew that now.

He didn't purposefully deceive Emily, but he'd deceived himself. He said he trusted God, but had he? Had he really?

Even after a positive counseling experience that he thought had helped him put his family's rejection behind him, he still didn't trust God. Not when it came to women. To a relationship.

He'd ignored every woman God had put in

his life since then. Plain and simple, he wasn't actually over his parents' betrayal, and he'd decided he wasn't about to put himself in a similar position with a woman. Not once had he asked God what He wanted for his life. He'd prayed for Emily's safety, but asking if God wanted her in his life? Not so much.

He glanced at her, felt the pull that was between them and wanted to think that now that she knew about his money it didn't matter. But as he'd expected once he told her, he couldn't be sure.

Do You want me to be with Emily?

A knock sounded on the front door, cutting through the room.

He came swiftly to his feet, his hand drifting to his weapon, all his thoughts focused on the door. "You expecting anyone?"

She shook her head.

"Stay here and I'll see who it is." He strode to the entry and glanced out the side window, surprised by his visitor.

"It's Jake," he told Emily. "You can relax."

But with the look in Jake's eyes, the last thing Archer would do was relax. In fact, every defensive bone in Archer's body sat up and paid attention as he stepped outside and closed the door.

"What's wrong?" he asked in way of greeting.

"We finally got through the data on Oregon bow-hunting licenses," Jake said, trying to sound at ease but failing miserably.

The sick feeling in Archer's gut intensified. "And?"

"Fannon's an avid bow hunter and so is Lance Taylor."

"Can't say as I like to hear that, but I'm not surprised about Fannon." Archer looked around the property—for what, he didn't know, but his unease made him jumpy.

"Sounds like you're liking him for this?"

Archer told Jake about his visit to Fannon. "If he's good for starting the fire, then why not the arrow?"

"I can ask around his neighborhood to see if anyone can verify he was home during the fire, but getting the DVR information will take a warrant. As much as you suspect him we still don't have probable cause for a warrant."

"Then we need to find something," Archer insisted.

Jake quirked a brow. "How do you propose we do that?"

"Carothers will try to get Fallon to turn over his shoes so they can compare them with the print, but now that we know he's a bow hunter, let's start by asking for his alibi for the day he or someone else shot the arrow at Emily."

"I can pay him a visit," Jake offered.

"No," Archer said quickly. "I want to see his face and gauge his sincerity."

Jake eyed him for long moments and Archer felt like squirming in his boots. His pal had a way of seeing deep inside and he used it to make good decisions for the team. Archer usually appreciated it, but right now, he could do without it.

"Not a good idea, bud," he finally said. "You're too invested in this and might spook Fannon."

"You're right, but I don't trust Carothers to get Fannon to talk."

"Then I'll go see Fannon." Folding his arms across his chest, Jake leveled him with a look. "You do trust me to get it done, right?"

"Yeah. I mean, if I can't be there, you're a good alternate."

"Thanks for the vote of confidence." Jake laughed.

Archer had no desire to smile.

"I'll visit Taylor." Archer held up a hand. "Before you say I'm too invested, Taylor's a long shot, and I can handle him."

"Fine, but don't screw it up." Jake's phone rang, stilling his laughter. He pulled it from a holder on his belt.

"It's Carothers." He answered and listened intently, his free hand flexing, then curling into a fist. "You're sure?"

Archer heard Carothers's raised voice come through the phone but couldn't make out his words.

"Sorry, man. You're right. I was out of line." Jake sounded sincere, but he rolled his eyes as he continued to listen. "Thanks for letting me know." He ended the call and stowed his phone.

"What was that all about?" Archer asked.

"Stan Fannon. He just stopped by County for a visit with Withrow."

"Interesting." Archer paused to ponder the implications. "You think this means Fannon was in on the mall shooting, too?"

"Maybe." Jake shoved his hands in his pockets. "Another line of questioning I can use when I meet with Fannon."

Archer could already envision the questions and Fannon's response. His voice would sound much like Carothers's had. "Hey, why'd Carothers bite your head off?"

"He was at the jail questioning Withrow so he personally saw Fannon arrive. I asked if he was sure, more as a shocked response, and Carothers took it personally. Told me he was a good detective and there was nothing wrong with his vision."

"Touchy, much?" Archer shook his head. "Did he mention if anyone overheard Fannon and Withrow's conversation?"

Jake shook his head. "But Carothers hung around and then followed Fannon. He was dumb enough to head over to Withrow's house and he started to break the seal Carothers had put on Withrow's place."

"Carothers arrest him?"

"No. Fannon spotted Carothers and stopped short of tampering with the seal. Carothers believes, and I tend to agree with him, that there's something in Withrow's place that he doesn't want us to find so he sent Fannon to get it."

"I don't suppose you can insist that we get a chance to search Withrow's house, can you?"

"I not only can, but that's exactly what I plan to do." His gaze was hard and held a warning.

Archer sensed something difficult to hear was coming next. His throat was tight. His gut ached. He wanted to pace to get rid of the feeling, but he stood waiting instead.

"You know better than I do how guys like Withrow can behave once they experience the power of gunning someone down and taking a hostage can bring. They get a taste for it and it suddenly defines who they are and they want more of it."

"And…?" Archer prodded, wanting Jake to get to his point.

"And you also know that once they get this

taste they crave it. Like a drug. The only way Withrow can fulfill his craving—"

"Is through Fannon," Archer interrupted once he understood where Jake was going with this. "With Withrow living vicariously through Fannon, Withrow's going to keep after Fannon until he succeeds in ending Emily's life."

SIXTEEN

Emily had woken up cranky and a visit to Lance first thing in the morning wasn't improving her mood.

He sat behind the desk in his office decorated in a modern style of clean lines and bold colors. He wore a tailored suit and his expensive Italian shoes were propped on the desk. Emily stood in front of him, Archer at her side. Neither of them had accepted Lance's offer to sit, as they wanted to keep the upper hand.

Archer had asked to be in charge of the meeting, and she'd agreed, but would ask questions if she thought they needed asking.

"To what do I owe the pleasure of your visit?" Lance asked, that same phony smile that made Emily nauseous every time she met with him plastered on his face.

"We need to know your whereabouts at the time of the fire," Archer said, his voice deep and intimating.

"You suspect me of setting the fire," Lance said, a big politician smile sliding across his face. "That's priceless, but I have an alibi. My wife and I came to the fund-raiser together, and except for the few moments I spoke with you, she was with me all night."

"Your wife," Emily repeated. "That's your alibi? A woman who would lie for you."

"Now, don't go disparaging my wife," he said, but there was no bite in his tone.

"Where were you on the fifteenth of June?" Archer asked.

Lance arched a brow, but didn't comment. He dropped his feet to the floor and flipped through a planner on his desktop. "I was in Portland that day. All day, at a development conference."

"And I suppose you have someone who can vouch for you?"

His eyes creased and he appeared uncomfortable for the first time since Emily had known him.

"Why do you want to know?"

"Are you a bow hunter?" Archer asked curtly.

"Yes, but I fail to see—"

"Did you go hunting on the fifteenth?"

"No, as I said I was in Portland all day. Besides, hunting season isn't open in June. Despite what you're hinting at, I don't break the law."

"Then you won't mind giving me the name of someone who can confirm your alibi."

"I can provide a name if the authorities require it, but I'd rather not do so now." He stood, his eyes like ice. "Now, if you'll excuse me, I have an appointment."

Emily wanted to argue, but Lance made it clear that he wasn't going to share a name, and with no official standing in this investigation, Archer couldn't force Lance to comply. She suspected Archer's only recourse was to have Carothers interview Lance.

She started for the door, but Lance called out, "Remember, Emily. My offer to buy the B and B still stands, and I'm prepared to pay top dollar."

She turned to tell him no when he grabbed a sticky note and jotted something down, then held it out. Curiosity got the best of her, but she wouldn't let him know that. Without looking at what was likely a very enticing offer, she crumpled the paper into a ball and dropped it on his desk. "I said it's not for sale."

His eyes flashed with anger. He circled the desk, and advanced on her. "I won't take no for an answer."

Archer planted his feet on the floor between them as he'd done with Stan. "I'd stand down if I were you."

Lance ran his gaze over Archer as if he

thought he could take Archer in a fight. Archer widened his stance and eyed Lance.

Lance held up his hands and backed off.

"Answer one thing for me before we go," Archer said casually. "If you think Birdie's B and B is in such bad shape, why do you want to own it?"

Lance dropped into his chair, leaned back and clasped his hands behind his head. "I have plenty of cash to revitalize the place. Once I do, I'll have a monopoly on lodging establishments along the highway." He looked happy. Or at least that's what he wanted them to think, but something about his behavior put Emily on alert.

"You'll never have that monopoly," Emily said. "I'd rather bulldoze the place down than let you take over and make it a clone of your other properties."

She stormed out, her emotions roiling.

The minute they sat in the car, Archer faced her. "I'm sorry if I overstepped my boundaries in there. I know you don't like it when I interfere, but it's instinct with me."

"Let's just get going, okay?" she said, her thoughts still on Lance. "I don't want to sit here a minute longer."

Archer got them on the road. Emily pushed Lance from her mind and stared out the window at the familiar drive. They reached the road leading to the B and B, and a movement in the woods on the side of the road caught her attention.

She shot up.

"What is it?" Archer asked, alternating his gaze with watching the road and scanning the area.

"I thought I saw someone, but I guess I was wrong. Was likely just a branch." She sat back and waited for her heart to stop pounding.

A loud crack snapped through the air.

"Gunshot," Archer shouted. "Get down."

A bullet? Really?

Before she could process it, an explosion sounded from under the car.

"He hit the tire," Archer said. "Blew it out."

The vehicle fishtailed and swung wildly. Emily sat up to look as the car shot across the road, racing toward a steep ravine.

She screamed, and when the crash appeared imminent, she braced herself to shoot over the edge and die.

Archer's instincts told him to reach out and protect Emily, but he needed to keep both hands on the wheel to fight the blowout. He battled hard, but he couldn't gain control.

They plunged into a steep ravine, racing over scrub and ferns. Bumping over ruts.

The right tire hit hard, sending the vehicle airborne. His body slammed back against the seat, then his air bag exploded, curling over the wheel. The cloth bag slapped him aside the head, and he felt like his brain was a soccer ball at a World Cup match.

The car rolled. Tipping. Falling.

He fired a quick look at Emily. Her bag had deployed, too, and he couldn't see her.

"Hold on, honey," he rasped and braced himself for a hard landing.

He tried to reach for her, to protect her, while keeping his wits about him as the car somersaulted as if in slow motion. Over once. Over again. And again.

They came to land on the roof, the impact jarring him in his seat, his seat belt ripping into his chest. The windshield and side windows folded into catacombs of safety glass, and the vehicle compacted as if a big salvage yard crusher had them in its jaws.

He held his breath and waited for it to squeeze the life out of him. Out of them. The metal frame groaned but held and retained most of its shape.

He punched the bag from his face and stared at Emily. She was still hidden behind her bag. His chest went tight and realization hit him like a fist to the chest. He'd been so worried about letting Emily into his life that he'd missed the fact that he'd already come to care for her.

"Emily, are you all right?" he called out and recognized the panic in his voice as he clawed at the bag in her face.

"Yes," she said, her voice small and terrified.

He freed her from the fabric, his heart soaring when he confirmed that she was indeed alive and not seeming worse for wear. He gently cupped the side of her face, which was blistering red from the air bag. "Are you hurt?"

She stared blankly ahead. "My right leg hurts a bit. And my head."

After having just suffered a concussion, the force of the jarring air bag could put her at greater risk for a serious head injury. He took a moment to run an assessment of his own injuries to be sure he could help her down without further impact to her head. He also checked his sidearm and then listened for anyone approaching the vehicle.

"Let me call this in, get out of my belt, and then I'll come help you."

He made the call to 911 and notified Jake, then prepared to move. He heard Emily shift. "I know you can do this on your own, but please. Please, honey. Let me help you."

"Okay." Her voice was still small and shallow.

He mentally prepared himself to release his

belt and land on the crushed roof. He didn't feel any injuries now, but shock could be masking them and a drop to the roof might be the first indication. Too bad. He was going to get out and help Emily no matter what.

He reclined his seat so he'd fall into a prone position, unclipped the belt and mitigated the impact with his hands.

Pain radiated up his arms, but he ignored it and shimmied to release his legs and then kick out the remaining window glass. He maneuvered around until he could slip out the window, then stood, taking a look at the scrub to get his bearings and making a cautious search for the shooter.

A wave of dizziness assaulted him from being upside down, but he ignored it and moved around the vehicle. He ripped off his shirt and wrapped it around his arm to clear the glass from the passenger window while keeping his senses tuned to the area in case of another attack.

Emily dangled from her belt, her legs wedged up under the dash.

"I'm going to crawl in under you before you release the belt," he said. "So I can lessen the impact when you fall and you won't bang your head again."

He didn't wait for her response but eased his

upper body inside the car. A shard of metal cut into his back and sticky oozing blood seeped through his shirt, but he rolled and knocked the metal away with a fist and then peered up at Emily. He ran his gaze over her body, checking for blood. Her arm had sustained minor cuts, but no major bleeds.

Thank You, Lord!

He quickly assessed the situation, then smiled to help her relax. "You didn't have to go to such extreme lengths to get this close to me."

She smiled wanly, worrying him about her state of mind. It would probably be better for her health to leave her in the car and go for help so a medic could restrain her head, but whoever fired that gun could end her life while he was gone. He wouldn't let that happen.

"Okay, time to move. First I'll recline your seat so you don't jackknife and injure your legs." He wiggled in farther so he was centered under her upper body and braced his hands under her shoulders. "When you click the belt you're going to free-fall onto me, but I'll control the descent of your upper body."

"I could hurt you."

"If a little bit of a thing like you could hurt me by falling on me, I'm in the wrong line of work." He chuckled to elicit a smile from her, but all he received was a hint of one.

"On three, okay?"

She nodded, then winced in pain.

"One. Two. Three."

The click of her belt echoed through the car. The full weight of her body strained his arms, but he controlled her free fall. He slowly, very slowly lowered her down, their eyes meeting and holding. He saw the fear race across her eyes, then evaporate and heat up with awareness of him. Maybe reacting to the same look in his eyes.

Was she thinking the same thing? They could have died in the crash and would never have had a chance to get to know each other.

He felt something twang in his heart. An ache. A physical ache. Protectiveness mixed with a certainty that getting to know this woman was worth any pain or potential hurt he might feel.

Her eyes locked on his for a moment before she lowered her head and kissed him.

At the touch of her lips, fire raced through his body. He slid his fingers into her silky hair to draw her closer. To deepen the kiss. For a moment, he was aware of only her. Of the softness of her lips. Of the smell of her perfume. And then, a branch snapping outside had him ripping free.

He caught a flash of movement in the scrub. He didn't think, but rolled their bodies so he lay on top, protecting her. She didn't speak, just looked up at him. He shifted so he could see out the window. Boots, like the Nike's from the river footprint, and jean-clad legs whispered past them. He drew his weapon and aimed. The man kept moving.

"We have to take cover," he whispered. "I'll get out first."

He eased away, making sure to keep his body between her and the man. Archer slipped out silently and helped her down.

"Not a sound," he told her and gestured at a large tree where they could take cover.

He put her at his side, away from danger, and they slipped behind the tree. He tracked the man's movements. Archer wanted to go after the guy, but he couldn't leave Emily alone.

"You good to move at a quick clip…maybe run so we can tail this guy?" he whispered.

She nodded.

"Stay behind me. Hook your fingers into my belt and don't let go. That way, I won't have to look back to see if you're with me and can keep my focus on the guy. Okay?" He looked into her eyes to judge her readiness for this move.

She peered back at him, the strong woman he'd come to care for replacing the terrified woman in the car. "Okay."

He gave her a quick kiss on the forehead, then

turned and waited until she took a firm hold on his belt before setting off through the thick grass and brush. He moved stealthily to keep from alerting the guy, and he was thankful that she was able to move quietly, too. They walked for a mile, when the man suddenly took off running. His footfalls thudded hard as branches snapped.

He'd made them.

Archer couldn't run with Emily attached to his belt so he stepped up his speed as fast as possible with her remaining in the protected position. He'd rather lose the guy than risk her life.

They climbed steadily upward, heading toward the road. The weight on his belt tightened. Emily was tiring. He slowed, but kept them moving forward.

Archer reached the top of the incline. Paused behind a tree and peered down the road. He caught a flash of a black pickup whizzing away.

"Taylor had a fleet of black trucks outside his office," he said.

"But we just left him."

"Any way he could get ahead of us?"

She panted from the hike then, gained a breath. "If he knows the old logging roads around here, he could have taken them and beaten us here."

"Then we best get Carothers or Jake to haul

Taylor in for questioning," he said. "What about Fannon? You know what he drives?"

"I've seen him in a white van with his company logo on it."

"Sounds like a business vehicle. He likely has a personal vehicle, as well. I'll check DMV records after we talk with Carothers."

"I'm scared, Archer."

He snaked an arm around her shoulder. "I'm here for you."

"And I appreciate that, but…"

"But what?" he asked, narrowing his eyes. "You don't think I can protect you?"

"You're good at your job. I've seen that, but the guy driving that truck had to know that there was a good chance we'd die in the crash. Doesn't that mean he'd be willing to use the gun on me, too?"

"Do you want me to tell you what I really think?" Archer asked quietly.

"Yes, of course."

"I doubt that the shooter was trying to cause a blowout. There are too many factors he can't control. Like where the tire is pierced and the heat of the tire. Also the age of the tire can be a factor. Bottom line is he couldn't be sure his shot would work or just cause a leak in the tire."

"Unless he was an amateur and didn't know any of those things," she mused.

"You're right. We're most likely dealing with an amateur, but honestly—" he reluctantly met her gaze, hating what he was about to say "—the incidents have been escalating, and I'm more likely to believe he's a bad shot and that bullet was actually meant for you."

SEVENTEEN

Emily had been under house arrest all day, so she took the time to do paperwork while Carothers and Jake continued to try to locate the shooter. Archer sat across from her, staring at his laptop. House arrest was Archer's plan to protect her. She was to remain inside at all times and away from windows. And whenever possible, under his watchful gaze. The gunshot terrified her, and she gladly listened to him.

Not that he was paying much attention to her right now. He kept his focus on his laptop. Unfortunately, that gave her time to watch him unobserved and think about the latest kiss. She didn't know what possessed her to kiss him. Maybe it was the fear of dying and the relief of surviving. But she was over that now, and if she was honest with herself, she had to admit that she'd gladly cross the room right now and kiss him again. And again.

He'd enjoyed the kiss, too. That wasn't a secret and she suspected he'd gladly repeat it. Not good. Not when she was confined to the house with him.

The only way she could make sure that it didn't happen again was to tell him that the kiss was a knee-jerk reaction to the stress and that it meant nothing. Neither did the first one. After all, she hoped that was all it was.

The moment he looked up, she said, "I need to talk to you about what happened earlier." The words tumbled out of her mouth, as she wanted to get this over with.

He arched a brow, his expression unreadable. "I assume you mean when you kissed me."

"Yeah, that," she said. "I shouldn't have done it, and I don't want you to read too much into it. I was upset. You comforted me. I kissed you in the moment as a response to your care and consideration."

He sat silently watching her. She could almost see thoughts running through his brain like the scroll on the bottom of a TV news program.

"I mean, we're going to be together in the house for who knows how long and I want to make sure we're on the same page here and it doesn't happen again."

He frowned, then gave a firm nod. "I understand. Let's forget it ever happened."

Surprised at his easy acquiescence, she sat

back, feeling oddly disappointed. She didn't know what she expected him to say, but maybe she'd hoped he would tell her the kiss had meant a great deal to him. She'd kissed him in the moment as she'd said, but her reaction to his response told her it ran deeper than she thought.

So what? Even if she could now see that having a man in her life might be a blessing, finding a way to care for and support Birdie had to come before anything else.

Deftly switching gears, Archer tapped his computer. "I was just about to pull up Fannon's DMV record to see if he drives a black truck."

"Then by all means finish it and tell me what you find."

He clicked the mouse a few times and his gaze sharpened. "Like you said…he has a white Ford van registered to his electrical business. But he has another vehicle, too. He drives a Ford F150 pickup." He looked up from the computer. "Color…black."

"Stan ran us off the road. Really?"

"There's a good likelihood. Him or Taylor. We'll just have to wait for forensics to process the bullet and hopefully it will match a weapon owned by one of these men." Archer closed his laptop and pushed back from the desk. "But, I also need to mention that the truck we saw might not have anything to do with the accident. The shooter could have already departed in another vehicle."

"But you think it was Stan or Lance, right?"

"Yeah. I do."

"Dinner's ready," Darcie called from the hallway.

Archer came to his feet. "We should go eat."

"How can you think about eating at a time like this?"

He smiled, but it was halfhearted. "If you've ever had Darcie's roast beef and vegetables you'd understand."

When she and Archer were running for their lives, then giving their statements to Carothers, Darcie had held down the home fort and put a beef roast with onions, carrots and potatoes in the oven.

Emily doubted she'd be able to eat much, but she'd join them so she could spend time with Birdie. She trailed him into the dining room. As they sat down, the front door opened and Archer spun.

Jake stepped into the foyer and sniffed, a broad smile spreading across his face. He really was a handsome man. He was big and bulky while Archer was trim. At first, she hadn't recognized Archer's strength. He might look lean, but he was packed with muscle. And when the shot was fired and his arms had come around her? She'd felt safe. Really and truly safe. Much like the way she'd felt when she moved in with Birdie. Though, there was more with Archer. Way more. And it was time for her to admit it.

Didn't mean she had to do anything about it, but it was there. She cared about him and for the first time in her life, she could see the real value of a relationship.

Jake stepped into the dining room. "Am I too late?"

"No, you're just on time," Darcie said.

"Here, take my place. I'll get another plate for you." Emily grabbed another place setting from the kitchen and when she'd returned, they'd added another chair by Birdie so Emily took that seat.

"Do you want me to update you on my visit with Fannon now or wait until after dinner?" Jake asked from the end of the table.

"Now," Emily said, knowing he couldn't ruin her appetite any more that it already was.

"First, I talked with Carothers. While waiting for the confirmation of Fannon's alibi, Carothers talked to Fannon's neighbor, who remembers Fannon going out the night of the fire. Said Fannon left around eight, but he doesn't know what time he came home."

Archer set down his fork. "So he could have torched the place."

"Yes, plus he doesn't have an alibi for when the arrow was fired at you or for the night of your attack at the river."

"What about the boots?"

"Believe it not, he surrendered them to me, and I've got them in the car to deliver to Carothers."

"Are they the right size?" she asked.

He nodded.

"Does he know that we lifted the boot print?" Archer asked.

"Yeah, I had to tell him to get him to hand over the boots."

"Then the fact that he did leads me to believe he isn't the one who shoved you into the river."

"So we could be looking at Lance," Emily said, her mind adjusting to a new suspect.

"First things first," Jake said in a low tone. "Let me get the boots to Carothers. If they're not a match, I'll stop by Taylor's place tomorrow to have a talk with him. And then we'll go from there."

"That will work," Archer said, and Emily could tell it was taking all the patience he could muster not to race out the door and confront Lance himself.

The following morning passed quickly as Emily sat quietly in her office and worked on the mound of paperwork for the B and B piled high on her desk for weeks. She'd been keeping an ear out for any sign that Jake had called or stopped by to tell them what they'd discovered about Stan's boots.

A slamming car door grabbed her attention. Archer was in the living room so she took a quick peek through the window. The man walking toward the house was dressed in a black suit, red tie and white shirt. Most important, he was a stranger.

Archer came to the doorway. "You know the guy coming up the walk?"

"No."

"Then move away from the window, and I'll go check him out." He stood looking at her and she suspected he was waiting for her to comply.

She returned to the desk. He pivoted, and she heard his footsteps receding across the floor. The front door opened, then a short conversation followed before it sounded like Archer had let the man into the foyer.

Most curious. She got up and waited for him by the doorway.

His eyes were narrowed, but she didn't get a dangerous vibe from him so she relaxed.

"His name is Melvyn Yancey. He's from the bank and needs to talk to Birdie."

No danger, but if a banker came to make a

personal visit, it couldn't be good. Or maybe she was thinking along the wrong lines here. He could simply be checking in. A personal visit like this would never happen in Portland or another big city, but in small-town America, it wasn't uncommon for a banker or insurance agent to stop by instead of sending a letter or picking up the phone.

Feeling more at ease, she stepped into the entryway. She saw Darcie sitting on the sofa in the living room, a frown on her face. Emily met Darcie's gaze, and she smiled, but it wasn't her usual bubbly smile. Her expression brought back Emily's concern about what the banker had come to say.

"Mr. Yancey." She introduced herself and they shook hands, but she didn't offer him a seat until she had an idea of what the visit was about.

"Is your aunt joining us?" He glanced around. "I was hoping to speak to her in person."

"She's resting, and I'd hate to wake her," Emily said. "I've taken over managing the business so perhaps this is something I can handle."

A sour expression puckered his face. "I'm afraid it's bad news so I'll come right out and say it. Unless Birdie can bring her account current by the end of the week, we'll be filing papers to repossess the property."

Not as bad as she thought. They probably

hadn't credited the mortgage payment she'd made yet. "I made an online payment yesterday. When that posts, we should be fine."

"Was the payment for the full balance?" he asked.

"No, but we're only two months in arrears, and I was told as long as we don't go ninety days, we'll be okay."

"I have no idea who told you that, but in addition to the number of months delinquent, we also look at the payment history. Birdie has been struggling for six months now with no sign of rectifying the situation." The banker paused and took a deep breath. He appeared as if he was honestly struggling to deliver this news. "I reviewed this issue with your aunt on the phone a few weeks ago, but it sounds like she didn't tell you."

Oh, Birdie. Did you forget or did you not want me to worry?

"She's had some issues with memory lately. Perhaps since she didn't give me the message, you could hold off on the proceedings so I can figure a way to bring our account current."

"I'm sorry, Ms. Graves. It's out of my hands now. I've known Birdie for years and feel bad about this. Truly I do. That's why I wanted to come by and give her a heads-up before a stranger served the foreclosure documents."

Emily should be thanking him for giving them a chance to fix this, but she couldn't embrace that right now. Not when he was going to take her home.

Tears clawed at her eyes and she didn't know what to say. What to do. The B and B and Birdie had been the only constants in her life, and she was losing both of them far faster than she expected.

Panic nearly stole her breath.

She looked at Archer, begging for his help. Not monetary help, but for his comfort. He didn't respond, but remained at the doorway frozen, like an ice sculpture, and didn't give her even a hint of what he was thinking.

She was surprised, but she didn't know why. It was just what she expected from a man. All the men she'd lived with growing up proved that when the going got tough, men bailed.

Why had she ever thought Archer was different?

Because you care about him. Too bad, because all you're going to get for the caring is a broken heart.

Archer remained in the foyer, unable to move. Emily's acute pain cut through his heart. It had been tearing him up since the banker made his announcement, then had taken off. Continued when Birdie came down the stairs and Emily told her about the banker and then curled into a stuffed chair in the family room looking like a waif without a home. Birdie wavered between understanding and confusion so she was no comfort to Emily. In fact, her nonsensical talk was likely making it worse. Darcie simply sat and stared at him.

He could hardly stand by and not do something, but after the way Emily had reacted to their kiss, reacted each time he'd gotten close to her, he doubted she'd want his interference in a personal matter now.

Darcie approached him, looking disgusted. "Seriously, Archer. Can't you see she needs you? So get over whatever hang-up has your feet planted out here and go help her."

Did she need him? Did she really?

"Now, dude," Darcie said.

"But Birdie," he replied, using it as an excuse. "In the state she's in, she doesn't need to hear any more about the foreclosure."

"Don't be such a chicken." Darcie thumped him on the head. "I'll take Birdie on a walk so you two can be alone."

Darcie crossed over to Birdie, and after she finally got Birdie's attention, she convinced her that a nice walk would be a good idea. Darcie took the older woman's elbow and escorted her toward the door. As Darcie passed, she gave Archer the stink eye.

Okay fine. He *was* being a chicken. He didn't want to hear Emily tell him to go away again. To reject his help. So what? If he really cared about her, he'd do this. He talked people out of killing other people. Out of killing themselves. Surely, he could man up and tell a woman he cared about that he was here for her.

He went into the room. She glanced up, then looked away.

He approached the chair and squatted next to it to gain her focus. "I'm sorry for the bad news, honey."

She swiped away a lone tear rolling down her cheek. "This is the end of the B and B. Really and truly the end."

"Like I mentioned before, I can lend you the money you need," he said with sincerity. If she took him up on it, he'd have to determine if she had true feelings for him or if she was after his money, but right now he'd give anything to take away her pain. Even a potential future relationship with her.

"No," she said firmly and shook her head.

He knelt to move closer and took her hand. "It's no secret that I have feelings for you, right? I mean I've been pretty obvious about it, and it hurts to see you so upset when I can make all of this go away. I want to help, Emily. Please let me."

"I've already said no, Archer, and I won't change my mind." Her tone was stern but she didn't remove her hand.

He took that as a positive sign and continued. "If you won't take my money, then let me be here to support you as you work through this. And then…"

"Then what?" She snatched back her hand and shot to her feet. She paced, her back to him.

He got up, too. "Then if you feel the way I do, we can…you know. Start dating or something."

She spun on him. "Even if I admit I feel something—"

"You do?"

"Fine, I do," she blurted out. "But can't you see it makes no difference? My life is falling apart around me. I can't get involved with anyone. I'm soon going to be homeless while caring for an aunt with Alzheimer's."

"I can help with that, too."

"Maybe you could, but even if my life was a bed of roses, I'm not getting involved with you or any guy."

"Why?" he asked bluntly.

"Why? You want to know why?" She crossed her arms and breathed hard. "Because my mother taught me about relationships. They're great at first. Then the truth is revealed and it all falls apart and she gets hurt. Time after time she proved it to me, and I'm not going down that path. Not ever." Emily shook her head. "Now, if you'll excuse me, I have paperwork to complete."

Archer shoved his hands through his hair and exhaled roughly. He didn't know what to say. What to do. Not when she was being so impossibly stubborn.

He saw Darcie and Birdie outside. He'd join them on their walk and hopefully it would clear his mind and he'd cool down.

A car came up the driveway just as he stepped outside and down the stairs. His hand went to his weapon, but then he recognized Ralph Inman behind the wheel. He parked and got out.

"Emily in?" he asked. "I wanted to give her the deposit slip from the fund-raiser."

"She's in the office," Archer said and watched the older man go inside before he joined Birdie and Darcie down by the garden.

He'd always imagined the day he'd meet a woman who didn't care about his money. A woman he was totally and completely attracted to, but never in his imagination did the woman tell him to get lost and run out of the room.

EIGHTEEN

From the office, Emily heard the screen door close and Archer storm outside. She'd hurt him. Hurt herself, too. She wished she could let go of her past. To embrace her feelings, but it was impossible to forget the years when she'd been schooled the hard way on relationships.

She heard footsteps in the hallway. Maybe he was coming back. Her heart sped up and she waited with anticipation.

Ralph poked his head around the corner.

"Oh, it's you." She tried not to sound disappointed, but from his expression, she hadn't managed it very well.

"Don't sound so excited to see me." He laughed.

"Sorry. I thought you were someone else."

He set his ever-present satchel on the desk, drew out an envelope and handed it to her.

She figured it was more bad news, so she forced herself to open the envelope and peek inside. It held a deposit slip from the fund-raiser.

Something she would have taken joy in seeing a few hours ago, but now a hysterical laugh fought to be released. She swallowed it down.

"I figured you'd want this for your records," he said, watching her.

She didn't know how to tell him about the bank so she'd just come out with it. "Thanks for bringing it, but as it turns out, the bank is foreclosing on Friday anyway."

"What?" His voice shot up. "No. I don't understand. You paid the mortgage, right?"

She filled him in on the banker's news, and he grew agitated as she talked. Not surprising. He'd put many years of his life into the business.

"I appreciate everything you've done for the B and B," she said, making sure he heard how sincerely grateful she was for his dedication. "But the bank has won, and it's time that I accept it's over. I need to find a new place to live as soon as possible."

"No!" Panic creased Ralph's eyes and he started pacing. "It can't be over."

He took rushed steps, his hand kneading muscles at the back of his neck. She got that he'd devoted his life to the business, but his reaction seemed over the top. Maybe he was worried about Birdie.

"It's okay, Ralph," she soothed. "I'll make sure Birdie is taken care of." *Somehow.*

He kept pacing, his gaze darting around the room. "This can't be happening. Not now. It just can't."

He stopped and stared at her but he wasn't seeing her. His gaze was unfocused and watery.

"Not now when I'm this close," he mumbled and started moving again only to stop and stare out the window.

"This close?" she asked, confused.

He pivoted and glared at her. This time his gaze connected with hers, locked into place and she didn't recognize the man staring down at her. His eyes had gone hard and mean, his nostrils flared in anger. He crossed to the desk. Shot a hand into his briefcase and came out holding a silver handgun. He aimed it at her.

"Ralph?" she asked in shocked amazement.

"I've put way too many hours into this place to let you, the bank or anyone else reap the rewards." His hand shook, but he continued to level the gun at her. "You know about the money, don't you?"

"What money?"

"Quit playing dumb, Emily. You're not dumb. I can see that from the questions you've been asking since you arrived." He nodded at one of his old ledgers sitting on the desktop. "You were just building your case. Asking all the right questions about the B and B's financial records, to prove I've been embezzling for years."

Embezzling? She stifled a gasp. The man she'd known for most of her life had been stealing from Birdie.

"How?" she asked.

"Really, this dumb act isn't working. You know about it. How'd you figure it out? Did you try contacting the vendors and found out they didn't exist?"

Was he saying he'd paid money to bogus vendors, then cashed the checks himself? If so, it was a common scheme that was nearly impossible to discover in a one-man bookkeeping situation. Especially with someone like Birdie who paid no attention to the books.

"I honestly didn't know," she replied carefully. "You know I haven't had a chance to review the old ledgers so there's no way I could have discovered it."

He pointed at an old ledger on the desk. "Then why is that one out?"

"I never put it away after our last visit when we reviewed the account for our emergency fund."

"I don't believe you." He tightened his grip on the gun. "But it doesn't matter now, does it? If you didn't know before, you do now."

"You can put the gun away," she encouraged. "I won't report you."

"I don't believe you, Emily, and even if you really do mean it now, I'm not going to sit around and wait for the day that you change your mind. I'd rather die than go to jail." His focus sharpened even more. "But my plan. I have to finish my plan first. I deserve the reward for all the years I put in here working for a pittance."

"What reward?"

"Lance, of course. I'm selling the B and B to Lance Taylor."

She gaped at him as she processed his second bombshell. "You have no authority to sell it."

"That's where you're wrong. I have power of attorney."

"How?"

"On one of Birdie's trips into la-la land I got her to sign it over to me." He laughed. "Wasn't hard. I told her to sign and had two of our suppliers witness it."

"Didn't they realize she wasn't of sound mind?"

"Once I told them that I was entering into a deal that would guarantee their account revenues would skyrocket, they didn't even care to ask."

Emily shook her head, but couldn't find words to say how disgusted she was with how the focus in the world had become all about money. Sure, she needed money to live on, to save Birdie's, but beyond that she could care less about money and all the trappings it could buy. They were just that. Trappings.

"Don't you think Lance will question your power of attorney?" she asked, though she already knew Lance would jump at the chance to own Birdie's and he probably wouldn't bat an eye.

"As badly as he wants it, are you kidding me? He isn't going to miss out on his big payday."

"Payday? Is that another one of your secrets?"

"Guess it won't hurt to tell you now. A major developer is quietly buying up all the land in the area so he can build a megaresort. Lance figures if he owns the remaining properties, the developer will offer big bucks to buy them." Ralph snorted. "Joke's on Lance, though, 'cause I'm gonna ask for more before I sell."

"You've been planning this for some time, haven't you?"

"Months and months. Then you had to show up, and Birdie let me go. So I did the only thing I could. I tried to make the business fail so you'd decide to take off with Birdie. Then I'd offer to take care of selling the property." He huffed a laugh. "I'd sell it all right. To Lance and line my pockets."

A dawning realization hit her. "You've been trying to kill me. It was you yesterday with that gun trying to shoot out our tire."

"Yes, but I can't take credit for all the other stuff. I suspect Stan or Delmar set the fire and shot the arrow at you."

"And the pot rack?"

He shook his head. "Not me. I thought it was an accident just like you did."

"Was it you who pushed me into the river?"

He frowned. "I had to. Don't you see? If you would have just given in and left town, I wouldn't have had to keep escalating things. I really didn't want to kill you. I had no idea you'd hit your head. And shooting the car? I just meant to scare you."

For some crazy reason she believed him. "But now? Why the gun? You said you're not really a killer." She reached out her hand. "Give me the gun, Ralph, and I won't tell anyone about this. Or press charges against you."

"No…maybe…" His eyes wavered for a moment. "I don't know. I need time to think. Time to figure out what to do. I can't let you go until I do."

"Archer's right outside, and he'll be in here soon," she said, hoping it was the truth.

Ralph's gaze shot around the room then landed on the door. "C'mon. We're going."

"You can't possibly think Archer will let you take me with him."

He shoved her toward the door. She lowered her shoulder and barreled into him. He wobbled. His arm shot out, knocking a painting on the floor. She took advantage of his imbalance to charge at him again.

He managed to step back and she crashed into the chair, sending it flying before she landed hard on her shoulder. She rolled and found him standing over her with the gun.

"Try that again or cry out, and I'll kill Birdie."

The anger radiating from his eyes said he meant it and filled her with terror unlike she'd ever felt before, so she got up and they walked to the door.

"We'll go the minute Archer turns his back. Down the steps and behind the car. Then get in the backseat and lie down." He jabbed her with the gun. "You got it?"

"Yes."

Ralph looked out the window. "Go! Now."

They charged out the door and down the stairs. She saw Archer, Birdie and Darcie, but Birdie was pointing at an old ship's anchor she'd bought at an auction and was likely telling them how she acquired it, so they missed seeing her or Ralph.

Emily resisted ducking behind the car, her focus on Archer, willing him to turn.

Ralph pushed her down, and with a boot to her chest, he held her there.

She stared at his boot. It was then that she remembered he'd liked the hikers that the club bought and had purchased a pair himself. He really was the suspect they were seeking, right here under their noses the whole entire time. Close, so close.

How had she forgotten the boots? How?

Her error might very well cost her life.

Archer tried to listen to Birdie's story about the anchor and appreciate the fact that she was once again in the present, but as he stared at the large anchor, his mind fully focused on his conversation with Emily. He couldn't believe he'd bared his feelings and she'd turned him down.

Point-blank, she didn't want a relationship with him. Her rejection crushed his heart as he'd known it would if he'd opened up to her. He'd seen the signs all along. Knew the potential was there because of her past, but he'd failed to heed his own common sense.

Never get involved. He knew that. Lived that.

Instead of paying attention to his past, he'd listened to Darcie of all people. A woman who'd found her true love and thought everyone could bask in that kind of happiness. Not him. Life had repeatedly told him that, and he'd finally gotten it through his thick head.

The only bright point was that his money had no importance to Emily. A meaningless victory.

His phone rang and he was grateful for the distraction. He spotted Detective Carothers's name on the screen and answered.

"We processed Fannon's boots," Carothers said. "They're not a match."

"Not a match?" Archer exclaimed, drawing Darcie's and Birdie's attention. "That's impossible. Maybe he has another pair."

"We searched his house. If he has a second pair, he's discarded them. Plus he has an alibi for the time and it checks out."

"Okay, so Lance Taylor, then."

"Could be, I suppose," the detective said, "but I just don't see him resorting to firing at Emily just so he could own the B and B."

"Maybe his finances are a mess and owning the B and B somehow helps him fix it."

"Now you're just reaching for anything."

Archer hissed out a breath, trying to rein in his anger and frustration. "Then who in the world is doing this?"

"I don't know, man, but our soil test was a bust, too. Nothing out of the ordinary."

He kneaded tight muscles in his neck. "So where do we go from here?"

"I still like Fallon for the fire. With boot prints not matching, I gotta figure he's working with someone else so I'm putting pressure on him, hope he'll crack and give up his partner. If he doesn't give me anything, I'll start with the rest of the Oregon Free members who own the Nike boots. Odds are it's one of them."

"Keep me updated." He disconnected his call and shoved his phone in his pocket.

"Uh-oh," Birdie said as she stepped over to him. "What's wrong?"

"Do you know about the boot prints we lifted at the river?"

She nodded. "Nikes I think you said."

"We thought that Stan Fannon had made the prints, but turns out the soles on his boots don't match the cast. So now we have to start over to figure out who pushed Emily."

"Maybe if you show me a picture of the boots I can help narrow down your search."

Archer doubted she could help, but he would try anything right now. He loaded the picture on his phone, then held it out for her.

She took a good look, then peered at Archer. "Oh, *those* boots. I guess there's something special about them. I remember when Ralph got a pair. It was like he was—"

"Wait," Archer said. "*Ralph* owns these boots? Are you sure?"

"Yes. Emily's group got them at a discount, and Ralph got in on the deal."

Archer shot a look at Darcie. "Ralph was at the house. He just left. Stay with Birdie."

He charged across the lot and up the stairs. The front door was open, and a sick feeling oozed through his stomach. He raced to the office and came to a screeching stop. The chair was turned over. The picture on the floor. A clear sign of a struggle.

Emily was missing.

Had Ralph taken her?

Archer bolted through the house, searching each room and calling out for her. Kitchen. Second floor. Third floor. Back down again.

Panic reared up and sat on Archer's chest, making it hard to breathe. "Calm down and think, man, think."

He had to find out where Ralph lived or where he might take Emily. He ran to the door and called out to Birdie and Darcie to join him in the office.

Archer raced in there, squatted by a metal cabinet and pawed through folders, looking for Ralph's personnel file. He wasn't surprised not to find one in such a small business. He heard footsteps at the doorway. Jumped to his feet and ran to the door.

"Emily," he yelled, but saw it was Darcie and Birdie.

"Emily's missing," he told Birdie. "I think Ralph took her somewhere. Do you know his address?"

She shook her head. "Not off the top of my head. It should be in—" Her eyes lit on something on the desk, and she pushed past him into the room. She tapped a worn leather satchel sitting on the desk. "Belongs to Ralph. He's never without it."

"Well, he is now." Archer ripped the bag open and drew out a sheaf of papers. In the middle of the pile, he spotted an official document, and he shot a look at Birdie. "You signed over power of attorney to Ralph?"

"No," she said.

He held out the document that not only gave Ralph power of attorney, but it also revoked an earlier one given to Emily. "Is this your signature?"

Birdie studied the paper for a long moment.

"Yes," she whispered. "He must have gotten me to sign at a bad moment. The witnesses are suppliers I trusted."

Archer's gut cramped hard. "So Ralph has ulterior motives and he has Emily. We need to find him now."

* * *

The cabin belonging to Ralph's grandfather was nothing more than a shack ready to crumble into the earth below tall pines. Emily had tried every argument she could think of to get Ralph to let her go, but when he tied her to the chair with smelly old ropes, she started to panic.

"Birdie needs me, Ralph. The Alzheimer's is taking a toll. Don't you care about her at all?"

"She doesn't have Alzheimer's," he said, crossing the cracked floorboards and waving the gun at her. "The doctors are wrong. She has substance-induced persistent dementia. I gave it to her."

"You what?" She stared at him openmouthed.

He grinned, but it was sick. "Months ago, I went up to the room Birdie is staying in to try to repair a leak that Birdie couldn't afford to get fixed. You know I'm a history buff, right? Well, I recognized the wallpaper in that room. It was designed by William Morris."

"And that's significant, why?"

"Morris included copper arsenate in the manufacture of his paper. When it becomes damp, it releases toxic fumes and people exposed to the fumes can develop toxic encephalopathy."

"Which is what exactly?"

He sighed as if she should understand. "It's a

neurologic disorder caused by exposure to toxic substance. It mimics Alzheimer's symptoms."

"And you got Birdie to move to that room, but why?"

"Lance Taylor had just offered a crazy sum to buy the place. Of course, Birdie said no, but you know what?" He shook his head in disgust. "I worked my tail off for Birdie, and the place was going to go belly-up. So why not sell it? I figured if I got Birdie to move into the room, and she lost her mental capacities, I could get her to sign over her power of attorney. Then I could sell the B and B to Lance and be set for life. So, I told Birdie to help alleviate financial difficulties that if she moved to the third floor, I could rent out her bedroom, too."

"And of course she did because she was desperate to see the business succeed." Emily's heart ached for her dear aunt being taken advantage of like this. "That was so low, Ralph. Lower than low. Preying on someone who paid your salary and treated you as family."

"Ah, but I'm not family, am I?" He closed the distance and pressed the gun against her heart. "You are, and even though you didn't care enough to stay and run the inn with Birdie, you'd inherit it while I slaved away day and night. I deserve to be compensated. But then you came home and ruined everything." He sneered at her, his lip curling up, and hatred radiated from his body.

Reality sank in.

If he poisoned Birdie in such a callous way, then there was no way he was going to let her live. Which left her with only one option.

She had to find a way to escape.

NINETEEN

Archer heard a car zooming up the driveway and went to the door. He immediately recognized Jake's SUV and Lance Taylor riding in the passenger seat. Jake slammed on the brakes, fishtailing to a stop. He jumped out and stormed around the car to jerk Taylor out.

Archer jogged down the steps. Birdie and Darcie followed.

Jake gave Taylor a shove. "Go ahead and tell him."

Taylor fired a testy look at Jake, but said, "I've got this big development deal in the works. I was with the developer at that June meeting I told you about. I figured you'd get curious about the meeting, check it out and find out he's planning a megaresort in this area. I've been quietly buying up land so I can resell it to him and make a lot of money on this deal. You asking for my alibi risked everything."

"Let me guess," Archer said. "Buying Birdie's property and reselling it is part of the deal."

"Yeah, and don't look at me like that. It's a legit move and I was going to give her a fair price."

Jake scowled. "Legit but underhanded."

"So why tell us about this now?" Archer asked.

"Your buddy here comes storming in the office." Taylor eyed Jake. "Claimed he had enough evidence to arrest me for attempted murder. I'm not going to jail for something I didn't do. So I had to tell him."

Archer gave Jake a look of thanks, then stared at Taylor, weighing, assessing.

He didn't squirm. Didn't back down. Didn't fidget. He was telling the truth.

Fat lot of good it did Archer. "That all you have to say? Because if it is, it wasn't worth the trip."

He looked up at Birdie. "You should know that Ralph is trying to sell the inn out from under you."

Birdie gaped at him, but Archer knew they were finally getting to the heart of the investigation. "Tell me everything you know about it."

"I made it a point to stop by here often. Just to keep raising my price and see if Birdie would bite." He shook his head, looked at Birdie. "You're a stubborn old girl."

"Not hard to be stubborn with the likes of you." She jutted out her chin.

"Continue," Archer said to Taylor to keep them moving forward.

"Last visit, Birdie stepped out of the room to get something and Ralph said he could make sure that Birdie sold. I asked him how, but he wouldn't talk about it where Birdie might overhear. I told him we could meet at my office. He said no. It's a small town and word would get around. So we arranged to meet at his grandfather's old cabin." Taylor laughed and shook his head. "The guy was all cloak-and-dagger when we could've met pretty much anywhere out of town."

At the mention of the cabin, Archer's interest picked up, but he wanted Taylor to finish the story before he started asking questions.

"Go on," Archer said.

"So we meet and Ralph tells me not to worry. He has everything under control. Birdie signed over her power of attorney and he was authorized to sell the place." Taylor's eyes narrowed. "But then Emily arrived and things changed. Ralph was furious, but he assured me she wouldn't be a problem. He'd make sure she went back to Portland, and Birdie's would be mine in plenty of time."

"Only one way Ralph could get Emily to go back to Portland," Jake said.

"Force her to go," Archer added, then glared at Taylor. "So this cabin where you met Ralph. Is it somewhere he might hold a hostage?"

"A hostage? For real?"

Jake jabbed Taylor in the arm. "Just answer the question."

"Yeah, I suppose. It's a falling-down old cabin that belonged to Ralph's grandfather."

"Can you tell me how to get there?"

"Sure, man. No problem." Taylor rattled off instructions, about ten miles down the road.

Archer didn't need to hear more, but held out his hand to Jake. "Your keys."

Jake shook his head. "You're too hyped up. I'll drive."

They charged toward the car.

Taylor cried out. "Hey, what about me?"

Archer hated leaving Taylor for Birdie and Darcie to deal with, but Archer had only one thing in mind. Emily's rescue.

Ralph had tried to call Lance but struck out and had to leave a message, thus buying Emily time. He paced around the room, mumbling plans, then changing his mind and going in a different direction.

"No!" He stopped and slapped his palm against his forehead. "My satchel. I was so focused on you that I left it at the B and B."

"Is that important?" she asked curiously.

"It has the power of attorney inside." He cursed under his breath. "I'll have to get it before I can make a sale to Lance. Hopefully everyone will be out looking for you, and I can slip in the back."

"And me?"

"You? Hmm…what do I do with you? I can't leave you here." He started pacing again, then spun and stared at her. "The trunk. I can put you in the trunk of my car. If you call out or make any noise, I'll make good on my promise to hurt Birdie."

Okay, so he was going to take her outside. Good. She could surprise him and make a run for the woods. He'd still have the gun, but she had to hope when it came right down to it, he wasn't a killer.

He untied her and gestured at the door. "C'mon. On your feet."

She stood slowly and stepped across the room. He came up behind her and put the gun in her back. She opened the door, hoping, no praying, that Archer, Jake or anyone for that matter would be standing outside to help.

She found no one.

Tears pricked at the back of her eyes, but she wasn't going to shed even one of them on Ralph. On the man she'd trusted for years. How could she and Birdie have been so blind?

He shoved her toward the car. She ran her gaze over the area. Found several tall trees where she could take cover. She remembered how stealthily Archer had moved through the woods after the accident. If she could make it safely into the woods, she could mimic Archer's moves and hide from Ralph.

They reached the trunk.

He dug keys from his pocket and pressed them into her hand. "Open it."

She slid the keys on the ring slowly, buying time.

"Quit stalling," he barked and pressed the gun harder, almost eliciting a squeal of pain, but she bit down on her lip to keep from crying out.

She inserted the key in the lock. Stepped back a fraction. Put her hand on the trunk to control the rate it opened. Inch by inch. Slowly she let it rise.

"Knock it off," he said and tried to swat at her hand.

He was unbalanced and the gun had dropped a fraction. Perfect time.

She threw her arm back, elbowing him just below the neck. He coughed and lurched.

She didn't look to see if he was incapacitated, she just ran. Hard. Fast. Over fallen pine needles. Through knee-high grass. Toward the trees. Not stopping. Step after step.

Three feet to safety. Two.

"Stop, Emily, or I'll shoot," he roared.

She heard the slider on his gun wrench back, but she was too close to stop now and kept going.

Archer charged into the clearing, but couldn't reach Ralph to take him down before he got off a shot.

"Ralph," he called to draw his attention from Emily.

The man spun. Archer prepared himself for a bullet, but when Ralph didn't fire, Archer held up his hands. "You don't want to shoot anyone."

"Fat lot you know," Ralph shouted. "It's my only chance not to go to prison."

"See, here's the thing," Archer said and pointed at the woods. "You can shoot me, but my buddy is standing right over there. If you take me out, he's gonna take a shot. You won't go to prison, but..." Archer let the implication register for a moment. "So why not hand over the gun and end this now? Sure, you'll serve some time, but you'll be alive."

"I don't know," Ralph said, his gun hand wobbling.

"Do it. Please, Ralph." Emily stepped into the clearing, her hands raised.

"No!" Archer shouted. "Get back behind the trees."

She shook her head and stepped toward them. "I know you're not a killer, Ralph. I know it."

He shook his head. "I have to. It's the only way."

"Then it's me you want, not Archer. He didn't do anything to you."

Archer lost his focus for a moment. Emily was offering herself in his place. He should have known she would do that and prepared somehow.

"I'm all yours, Ralph," Archer said, trying to gain control again.

Ralph glanced between the two of them, confusion on his face. "I—"

"Your decision is simple," Archer said quickly. "Shoot me now or give me the gun." He started walking toward him. Slow, small steps to see Ralph's reaction.

He didn't move. Didn't speak.

Archer kept coming. Normally he'd talk about people Ralph had to live for, who counted on him. To talk about the reasons Ralph had to live, but the guy was a loner, without much to look forward to other than travel to delve into his love of history. Without Birdie's money, he wouldn't be able to do even that.

A few feet from Ralph, Archer laid his hand out, palm up, and met Ralph's gaze. "Like Emily said. You're not a killer. Give me the gun."

He waffled for a moment then slapped it into Archer's hand. The cool metal felt better than most anything Archer had touched before. It meant he'd saved Emily.

Jake came out of the woods and strode across the clearing.

"Hands behind your back," he said to Ralph.

Ralph started weeping and complied without any issues.

Jake soon had him in custody. "I've already called for transport and we'll meet them out at the road."

"Thanks, man," Archer said and appreciated the fact that Jake knew Archer needed to be alone with Emily.

Emily swayed and looked like she might drop to the ground. He lurched forward and helped her take a seat on a nearby stump. She didn't speak but stared ahead, her expression unreadable. She'd just been through a fight for her life. For his life. And she hadn't shed a tear. Hadn't broken down. Just remained calm and sat looking ahead in a contemplative stare.

He squatted in front of her to gain her attention, but before blurting out the wrong thing, he took his time to seek the right words to tell her how much she'd come to mean to him. After all, the last time he'd tried it she'd shot him down. He couldn't let that happen again.

"Honey," he said, finally getting a response as she gazed at him.

When he expected to see fear, confusion, maybe anguish in her eyes, they were clear and focused. "I get it now. Finally."

"Get what?"

"What you were saying the other day. I can't control everything. I have to let go or it'll eat me up. If I want to live a full and rich life, I have to turn my life over to God. Really turn it over to Him. No matter His response to me. Silence or comfort. I will trust Him."

"I hear a *but* in your voice."

"But it scares me, you know? I've had a few hard knocks in life, and I'm just not sure if I can let go and risk living through more of them."

"I know what you mean."

"You?" She blinked hard. "You're the one who said it worked. To let go and let God."

"I did. I know. I thought I had." He dropped to his knees. "God was fully in charge until my parents turned their back on me. After that, I just mouthed the words. Said God was the boss, but never really let Him take over again."

"You were afraid of getting hurt again," she whispered. "I get it. Trust me."

"God does what's best for us, right? I knew that, but deep down I thought, what if He thought it best for me to be in a situation where I came to care for someone and they walked out, too? So I made sure not to put myself in those situations."

"But you did, with us," she added.

His heart was in his throat. He still feared her rejection, but he wouldn't run from it. He took her hands in his. "I tried to fight it. But I lost the battle. And now, seeing Ralph ready to shoot you, nothing mattered. Nothing but you. I want to get to know you. To start dating." He swallowed hard. "So what do you say, Emily? Are you willing to take a chance on me...on *us*?"

A soft smile played on her lips and she rested her hands on his shoulders. "Yes, I would very much like to see where these feelings take us."

"There's just one thing," he said, his old fears coming back. "The money. I have a huge pile of it in the bank. And if we get together, what's mine is yours, so why don't I give it to you now and you can save Birdie's?"

She shook her head. "Taking your money

would be a horrible way to start our relationship. If God wants us to keep Birdie's afloat, then He'll make the way. I just have to trust in that."

His heart soared with hope. "So you said *relationship*. I'm thinking such a big commitment should be sealed with a kiss." He didn't wait for a response but leaned closer.

"I think I'm falling in love with you, Emily Graves," he whispered.

"Me, too," she responded shyly.

He lowered his head and when their lips met, he knew their futures would be truly blessed.

EPILOGUE

Emily sat in the doctor's waiting room. Archer held her hand, and despite the fact that even after a few months of dating she still couldn't get enough of holding hands, right now she felt as if she would jump out of her skin if she didn't soon hear the doctor's prognosis for Birdie's recovery from the poisoning. Ralph was in jail for attempted murder and kidnapping, not to mention embezzling, and he'd likely never see the light of day again. And they located a video of Stan buying a gas can and he confessed to the fire and shooting the arrow. He sat in jail on charges of attempted murder.

The door opened and Birdie stepped out. Emily tried to read her aunt's expression, but she hid her emotions.

"We can talk about it in private," she said.

Emily didn't like the sound of that, but she followed Birdie into the hallway.

Birdie turned. "Doc says I'm rapidly improving, and he's more than happy with my progress."

"We already knew that," Emily said, waiting for more.

"Sorry, that's it. We just need to take it one day at a time and remember the brain damage could be permanent. Or now that I'm away from the poison, I could recover more of the functions I lost."

"You've already come a long way in two months," Emily encouraged. "I know it will keep getting better."

"Still not good enough to run the B and B and you need to get back to your own life, so I'm going through with selling the place directly to the developer." When they learned that Ralph had been embezzling and he had a large savings account, the bank agreed to wait for him to pay restitution and hold off on the foreclosure process.

"You're sure?"

"Positive. The proceeds will pay off my creditors and if I don't improve and require special care there will be enough money for that, too. If I improve enough to live independently, the money will support me."

Emily took Birdie's hand. "You don't have to worry about that. My new job in Portland is enough for us to live on and my new apartment is big enough for the two of us. You can live with me for as long as you want."

Birdie grinned at Archer and released Emily's hand. "I'm pretty sure this fine young man will have something to say about that."

Emily smiled shyly up at Archer. Being in a relationship was all so new to her, and she loved every minute of it. Sharing her worries. Her concerns. Taking and giving advice. Even arguing. And the kissing. She couldn't forget the kissing and being held by a strong man who would never willingly leave her.

"Emily's right, Birdie. Your needs have to come first." He slipped his hand into Emily's and put an arm around Birdie. "Let's get over to the firehouse for dinner." He led them down the hallway and to his car.

After Birdie's improvements, Archer had planned a celebratory dinner for the night. He said if they got bad news from the doctor, they could always cancel the dinner.

Archer helped Birdie into the backseat, but he didn't let go of Emily's hand except to run around the front and climb in, where he immediately took possession of it again and held it all the way into the firehouse.

Happy voices rang from the family room and she looked forward to joining Archer's friends. Her friends, too, now. She loved the sound of that.

"C'mon," Archer said, tugging on Emily's hand. "I'm starving."

They stepped into the room and Darcie came rushing over to Birdie. "Well, tell us. What did the doctor say?"

Birdie shared her news.

"That's good, then," Darcie said firmly. "I've noticed how much you've improved, and I know it will keep getting better." She looked at Emily. "You must be thrilled."

She nodded and worked hard to keep back the tears that threatened to flow.

"Okay, so, we're going to eat," Darcie said. "And then, I've got Krista, Morgan and Skyler—albeit she's going along with it unwillingly—to help me with some wedding planning. Are you game?"

"Of course," Emily said and wondered just how long it might be before she was planning a wedding of her own.

Archer watched Emily in the game room. She and the other women were gathered around bride's magazines, frilly lace, mints, flowers and other things that Archer had no idea what they were for. Birdie sat on the sidelines, but Emily kept drawing her into the conversation and she was having a good time, too. He and the guys had stayed well away from the wedding discussions, except Noah. He had no choice, though Archer had to say the beaming smile on his face said he was glad to help. The rest of them had been playing cards.

Birdie caught his gaze and stepped over to him. "She looks happy."

"With her wedding only a few months away, Darcie is on cloud nine."

"Darcie, yes, but I meant Emily." She smiled at Archer. "She's finally decided to live in the present, and I owe it all to you."

"I'd like to take credit, but all of it should go to God."

"You're right, but if you weren't such a fine young man, God wouldn't have put you in my Emily's life when she needed a strong man to lean on."

Archer liked to think the same thing, but it humbled him to hear Birdie say it aloud.

"And thank you for creating the Alzheimer's foundation in my name. Though I feel like a fraud as I don't have Alzheimer's."

"But you had—have—very similar symptoms so we all know what it's like."

"Except, thankfully I'm improving and I certainly won't get any worse."

"And we're all happy about that." He'd become so fond of her the past few months and was glad she traveled into the past less often.

She'd treated him more like a son than his real parents ever had.

He gave her a quick hug. "I'm glad my money is being put to good work."

Darcie suddenly jumped to her feet, grabbing his attention.

"I mean like this." She placed her back to the guys at a table behind the women and tossed the bouquet of flowers into the air.

The bundle of silk flowers flew end over end, tumbling and tumbling until suddenly starting a free fall near Jake.

Startled, he grabbed the bouquet before it hit him in the face and glared at Darcie. "What's going on?"

"I was just demonstrating my flower-throwing technique so Emily could be sure to grab the bouquet on my wedding day, but..." Darcie winked at Jake. "It looks like you're the next one up."

Jake scowled at them and Archer took pity on the guy. He was the only person in the group who hadn't found a perfect mate.

"Hey," Archer said. "Cut Jake some slack. He's been far too busy making sure we're all safe to have much of a personal life." Archer knew that wasn't the whole story, as Jake had free time. He just didn't date.

"Yes, well," he mumbled and tossed the bouquet back to Darcie, then he picked up his cards, "let's get back to it."

Archer hoped Jake worked through whatever was eating at him and he found the woman for him. Ugh, now Archer was sounding like Darcie.

So what? He couldn't be happier. He'd never imagined sharing a life with someone like Emily would be so rewarding. He'd seen everyone else succumb to love, but he didn't understand what it fully meant until now. With his parents as his role model, how could he?

But all of that had changed with Emily, and he intended to tell her that right now.

He took her hand and pulled her into the hallway. "It's been a good day."

"It has." She lifted her arms and wound them around his neck. "I'm so glad I moved back to Portland."

"You missed the city?"

"Actually, no. I like it at Birdie's, but you're in Portland and I want to be close to you."

"I want the same thing." He wrapped his arms around her and drew her closer. "You do know that no matter what happens to you or Birdie in the future, my money is yours from now on. I'll ensure that Birdie wants for nothing and is well taken care of for the rest of her life."

"Okay." Emily smiled.

"*What?* You finally agree?" He was surprised at how happy a woman taking his money made him.

"I'll never spend your money on myself, but you know I'll do anything for Birdie."

"So why didn't you accept before now?"

"Because I still thought I could do everything on my own." She smiled up at him. "Now I know it's so much better to let God take charge and have someone like you to rely on, too. Enough with this Lone Ranger business."

He bent closer, a mischievous smile on his lips. "Trust me, honey. You won't ever be alone again. I'll gladly be the Tonto to your Lone Ranger. But if you want to bring Silver into our lives, that we'll have to talk about."

She imagined Archer with a horse. Cleaning up after it, brushing it, just being in a smelly stall, and laughter came to the surface. But his lips descended on hers, ending her laughter and reminding her that no matter what came into their lives, with God in control, they were destined for great happiness and peace.

* * * * *

Dear Reader,

As I wrote the fifth book in the First Responders series, I was reminded of how much I like to try to control my world, much like Emily does in the book. I was raised by wonderful parents who wanted my siblings and me to be independent and self-sufficient. Good traits, except when you forget to ask God's will for your life and don't first rely on Him, or when you fear what His best might entail.

Near the end of the story, Archer comes to realize that though God does have our best in mind, deep down he feared that God might put him in a difficult situation that Archer would rather avoid. It could be painful and unpleasant. We try to avoid those kinds of situations, too, but it's in the messiness of life that God grows us stronger. So if you struggle with letting God take charge, I hope you'll remember Archer and Emily's story, where they learn that it's only in turning over their lives to God that they find His peace.

If you'd like to learn more about this series, stop by my website at www.susansleeman.com. I also love hearing from readers so please contact me via email, susan@susansleeman.com, or on my Facebook page, www.facebook.com/

SusanSleemanBooks, or write to me c/o Love Inspired, HarperCollins, 24th floor, 195 Broadway, New York, NY 10007.

Susan Sleeman

LARGER-PRINT BOOKS!

GET 2 FREE
LARGER-PRINT NOVELS
PLUS 2 FREE
MYSTERY GIFTS

Love Inspired®

Larger-print novels are now available...

YES! Please send me 2 FREE LARGER-PRINT Love Inspired® novels and my 2 FREE mystery gifts (gifts are worth about $10). After receiving them, if I don't wish to receive any more books, I can return the shipping statement marked "cancel." If I don't cancel, I will receive 6 brand-new novels every month and be billed just $5.49 per book in the U.S. or $5.99 per book in Canada. That's a savings of at least 19% off the cover price. It's quite a bargain! Shipping and handling is just 50¢ per book in the U.S. and 75¢ per book in Canada.* I understand that accepting the 2 free books and gifts places me under no obligation to buy anything. I can always return a shipment and cancel at any time. Even if I never buy another book, the two free books and gifts are mine to keep forever.

122/322 IDN GH6D

Name	(PLEASE PRINT)
Address	Apt. #
City	State/Prov.	Zip/Postal Code

Signature (if under 18, a parent or guardian must sign)

Mail to the **Reader Service:**
IN U.S.A.: P.O. Box 1867, Buffalo, NY 14240-1867
IN CANADA: P.O. Box 609, Fort Erie, Ontario L2A 5X3

**Are you a current subscriber to Love Inspired® books
and want to receive the larger-print edition?
Call 1-800-873-8635 or visit www.ReaderService.com.**

* Terms and prices subject to change without notice. Prices do not include applicable taxes. Sales tax applicable in N.Y. Canadian residents will be charged applicable taxes. Offer not valid in Quebec. This offer is limited to one order per household. Not valid to current subscribers to Love Inspired Larger-Print books. All orders subject to credit approval. Credit or debit balances in a customer's account(s) may be offset by any other outstanding balance owed by or to the customer. Please allow 4 to 6 weeks for delivery. Offer available while quantities last.

Your Privacy—The Reader Service is committed to protecting your privacy. Our Privacy Policy is available online at www.ReaderService.com or upon request from the Reader Service.

We make a portion of our mailing list available to reputable third parties that offer products we believe may interest you. If you prefer that we not exchange your name with third parties, or if you wish to clarify or modify your communication preferences, please visit us at www.ReaderService.com/consumerschoice or write to us at Reader Service Preference Service, P.O. Box 9062, Buffalo, NY 14240-9062. Include your complete name and address.

LILP15

Name	(PLEASE PRINT)	
Address		Apt. #
City	State/Prov.	Zip/Postal Code

Signature (if under 18, a parent or guardian must sign)

Mail to the **Reader Service:**

IN U.S.A.: P.O. Box 1867, Buffalo, NY 14240-1867
IN CANADA: P.O. Box 609, Fort Erie, Ontario L2A 5X3

WPBPA16R